BUG

The characters in this book are the sort of people the author has known all his life. But everyone in Tichburg is fictional, so we apologize to those who think they may recognize themselves.

The Adventures of Bug & Frogger

BUG

Frank B. Edwards

Illustrated by John Bianchi

🌿Pokeweed Press

Written by Frank B. Edwards
Illustrated by John Bianchi
Edited by Susan Dickinson
Copyright 2007 by Pokeweed Press

Cataloguing in Publication Data
Edwards, Frank B., 1952-
  Bug

(Adventures of Bug and Frogger)

ISBN 978-1-894323-17-8 (pbk.)

I. Bianchi, John   II. Title.   III. Series: Edwards, Frank B. 1952-
Adventures of Bug and Frogger

PS8559.D84F76 2007   jC813'.54   C00-900226-X
PZ7.E2535Bu 2007

Published by:
Pokeweed Press
Suite 337
829 Norwest Rd.
Kingston, Ontario
K7P 2N3

Printed in Canada by:
Friesens Corporation

Visit Pokeweed Press on the Net at:
www.Pokeweed.com

Send E-mail to Pokeweed Press at:
mail@Pokeweed.com

This book is dedicated to the children in my life — both young and old — who help keep me young and in touch with the things in the world that are really important: Kristen, Scott, Hayley, Emily and Kristin Jr.

Contents

A New Day

It was Bug's job to make breakfast on Friday mornings, and she was running late. Still in her oversized pyjama shirt and boxer shorts, she hustled about the tiny kitchen, moving quickly from cupboard to table, setting out bowls, plates and cutlery while keeping one eye on the time. It was 8 o'clock, and Walter, her father, liked to leave for work at 8:30. No time for coffee this morning.

She could hear Walter in the shower, singing a song from *The Wizard of Oz*:

"Follow the yellow brick road,

Follow the yellow brick road . . ."

He seemed stuck on that line, so she tuned out his cheerful off-key voice, convinced he was unable to finish the chorus because he didn't know the words. There was just enough granola for one more breakfast, and she made a mental note to mix up another batch this morning. She sawed two large slabs from the loaf of day-old bread she'd picked up at the Backdoor Bakery two days ago and dropped them into the toaster. Pouring herself a large glass of orange juice, she slipped onto one of the old, battered vinyl chairs to wait for the toast.

It popped up 90 seconds later as Walter rumbled into the room, humming tunelessly. His hair and bushy red beard were still wet, and instead of his work clothes, he was wearing a bagged-out old sweat suit, the legs and sleeves cut off for the hot summer weather.

"No coffee?" he asked, sniffing the air.

"No time today," answered Bug, grabbing the toast and dropping a piece onto each plate. "We slept in. My alarm didn't go off."

"Oh, we've got lots of time," said Walter. "I turned off your alarm before I went to bed last night. We've got plenty of jobs to do today, and they're going to be done on *our* schedule for a change."

He was grinning mischievously, a look Bug had come to dread. It meant Walter was up to something.

"What about work? Did they give you the day off?"

Walter was a salesman at a discount sporting-goods store — The Whole Sports Enchilada. Or he did yesterday, she thought, already beginning to imagine the worst.

"Ohhh, they gave me the rest of my life off, Bug, honey," Walter said happily. "Business is slow. Sales are down. The services of Walter Hapensak are no longer needed."

As Bug slumped deeper into her chair, he smiled down at her, still cheerful, then busied himself with the coffeemaker.

10

"Don't you worry, Bug. I've got a plan."

If he had *not* had a plan, Bug might have been less worried. At age 12, she was 25 years younger than Walter but felt that she was the more responsible of the pair. Walter's plans, though always interesting, were seldom successful — at least not in terms of the standard definition of success.

Looking across the ancient Formica table squashed into a corner of the small kitchen, Bug could only hope Walter's plan included a new job. No, not just a new job — a better job. But as she watched Walter squeeze past his old chair with its duct-tape patch on his way to the refrigerator, Bug thought he was way too happy to have a new job or a boss. And even before he started to explain his big plan, she knew he was going back into business for himself.

She braced herself as he moved cream, juice, jam and half a grapefruit from refrigerator to counter, waiting for him to sketch out his plan.

According to Walter, they had $1,000 in the bank — just enough to buy an old dump truck he had seen at a used-car lot around the corner . . .

Bug raised an eyebrow, indicating she was listening intently.

. . . and a friend of a friend who worked in a shoe company's warehouse had given him a line on the deal of a lifetime . . .

Bug frowned slightly, doubting that such a wonderful deal could exist.

. . . and as luck would have it, the shoe company had been clearing out its inventory of unsold shoes. After the discount-store buyers had taken away the good stuff, the firm still had a supply of 1,000 unmatched running shoes.

Walter beamed across the table at her, convinced he had delivered a plan that was so perfect, its merits would be obvious even to his unsmiling daughter.

"Unmatched running shoes?" Bug repeated.

"Yeah. It's great," Walter enthused, ignoring her look of disbelief. "These shoes are the leftovers from displays and factory mix-ups and returns from stores. The company can't sell them, and I found out yesterday that the shoes were going to be taken to the dump. Can you believe it? The warehouse manager was actually going to pay somebody $200 to haul them away."

"But he's not going to do that now because . . .?"

"Because I offered to take them off his hands for free."

"All right. So now you're unemployed, and we're going to spend all our money on an old truck, fill it with shoes that were on their way to the dump and . . . bring them home?"

"No, honey. This is where the real adventure begins," Walter explained. "Trust me, this is the best part."

Bug looked dubious. And nervous.

"We're moving — before we have to pay next month's rent, which would wipe out our savings anyway."

"Where are we going?"

"Away from the city."

"But where?"

"I haven't decided yet, but someplace nice, where we can get a little house and set up a business. You know. A great school for you. Good work for me."

"And we're leaving when? Next week?"

"Tonight, as soon as we get packed. I'm going to get the

truck this morning — I signed all the papers for it last night on my way home from the store — and, while I'm picking up the shoes at the warehouse, you'll stay here and pack everything in boxes. When I get back, we'll hit the road. No good-byes or fare-thee-wells. No regrets. The Hapensaks are on the move."

"Walter, what about me?" she protested, calling him by his first name, as she had since she was a toddler. "Dad" had never been part of her vocabulary.

"Bug, I'm doing this for you. We don't have a future here. You've been complaining for a year about having to go to junior high in the Flats. You haven't brought a friend home for two years.

"We don't have a life here anymore. We're barely surviving in this stuffy, cramped apartment. We're going to suffocate one of these days. The only thing I've got left is you — and a hunch that things are going to work out great."

"And don't forget our truckload of 1,000 pairs of shoes," Bug added.

"Not pairs, Bug. Single unmatched shoes. No two alike. Trust me, this is going to work out just great."

Moving On

After Walter left to pick up the truck, Bug worked furiously, emptying the contents of drawers and cupboards and filling the cardboard boxes that Walter had collected from a dumpster in a nearby alley. She was upset and frustrated, shoving socks and shirts and sheets into one box after another. But eventually, she calmed down enough to realize that this was a wonderful opportunity to get rid of everything in the apartment she didn't like.

The first items to go were the living room curtains and four of Walter's ugliest sportcoats. Bug shoved them into trash bags and hauled them down to the huge garbage dumpster behind the building. Then she got serious. Out went music tapes and CDs and cookbooks and bedspreads and all the sports posters tacked up on the apartment's dingy walls. If they were going to start over again, she thought, it might as well be with the things she liked. There would be no need for huge blowups of Larry Bird or Magic Johnson or the 1982 Harlem Globetrotters. She carefully sorted through the stacks of music tapes, preserving their favorites and tossing away anything they had not listened to for years.

As she was clearing out Walter's prized possessions, she wondered briefly what he would say when he discovered they were gone. He would be upset, but not for long. And there was always a chance that he might not even notice.

By the time Walter returned at 2 o'clock, everything they owned was either sealed up in a cardboard box or jammed into the garbage dumpster. The apartment walls were bare, the closets empty. Bug had left most of the food in the kitchen cupboards and refrigerator but had packed all their dishes and pots and utensils. Although none of these items were valuable, she had been eating and cooking with them as long as she could remember and wasn't about to leave them behind.

Walter was ecstatic at her speed and efficiency.

"I'm surprised you got all our stuff crammed into so few boxes," he said, surveying the 20 cartons stacked around the perimeter of the living room.

"I threw out some things we didn't need anymore," she admitted. "Like you said, we really didn't have a lot. What with starting over again and all, I figured it was time to clean house a bit."

They agreed to leave their furniture behind except for the beds, television and stereo. Nearly everything else had been second- and third-hand when they bought it five years ago — right after Walter's sports-card and autograph business had failed — and it wouldn't be hard to replace. Bug still held vague memories of an earlier time when they had lived in a much nicer place with new furniture, but since she'd been in grade two, their apartments had become smaller and darker and shabbier.

"Well," boomed Walter, "it's time to get this show on the road."

While he hauled cartons to the curb, each one tightly sealed with heavy-duty tape, Bug climbed into the back of the dump truck, wading through hundreds of colorful loose running shoes to try to organize their load. There was no hope of sorting through the huge mound of shoes, so she just scooped out a space in front of them to stow the boxes. While Walter shuttled from the apartment to the street, Bug stayed on the truck, moving boxes around and keeping an eye out for trouble.

It wasn't a bad neighborhood, but leaving a truckload of anything unattended was not a good idea, especially if you had banked your entire future on it. And Bug also had to look out for the landlord, who would not appreciate their sudden departure. Their rent was due in less than a week, and they were supposed to give two months' notice before moving, but Walter's inspiration did not allow for such financial complexities. He was anxious to leave without having to spend any more of their savings on the apartment.

As more boxes were handed up, Bug pushed them into the crater she had dug in the enormous pile of shoes, until everything was eventually crammed in. They heaved the two mattresses on top of the boxes, then pulled a brand-new plastic tarpaulin over the whole load.

Just as they were tying down the tarp, Chopsy, a local street person, ambled up to the truck to see what was going on. He was a cantankerous fellow who had befriended them when they moved into the neighborhood. Bug had been leery of him at first, but Walter had taken a liking to the man immediately, often giving him sandwiches and old clothing.

Chopsy was wearing a gold and black sportcoat of Walter's that Bug had just thrown out. "What the heck's going on?" he demanded. His language was usually laced with curses, but when Bug was present, he tried hard to keep a civil tongue.

"We're moving on, Chopsy," Walter said. "I lost my job yesterday, so we decided to get out of this city before it smothers us. Clean air and better prospects. That's what we're looking for."

Chopsy swore vigorously, then stopped and bowed to Bug.

"Sorry, Bugsy, couldn't help myself. You know how I love trees and farms and such. And chickens . . . oh, I love chickens. Grocery stores on legs, I calls 'em. Give 'em a bit of food every day, and they give you eggs right back. And when they stop giving you eggs, you don't have to feed 'em anymore cuz you can just eat 'em. That's right, you just . . ."

Bug began to tune Chopsy out, because when he started talking about certain things, there was no stopping him. He was a man of many passions who could ramble on for an hour or more about anything that popped into his mind, but Bug had never heard him go on about chickens before. She was brought back from her reverie when she realized he was changing topics.

"I'd come along with you if I could, but I can't — chickens or not. I've got a lead on a job next week, and I'll be able to buy all the chicken and eggs I want at the grocery store. My luck is changing, Walter. I can feel it in the air. I even found a nice jacket back there in the dumpster. Sort of makes me look like a car sales guy, don't it?"

"It looks good on you, Chopsy. I have one just like it," Walter said, glancing at Bug quizzically.

"Chopsy, we're leaving right now, and the apartment is empty, except for a bit of old furniture. The landlord is going to have to rent the place out right away, but if you want, you can use it until he kicks you out."

"I don't know," said Chopsy, considering the offer. "I've got a pretty nice setup now just under the Flatsview Bridge." He nodded his head toward Pollock Street, indicating his current address. "But it would be nice to have a bathroom and kitchen sink for a couple days. You got keys?"

Walter handed them over.

"You can have the furniture, if you want it. Just move it before the landlord does. He'll claim we owe him two months' rent because we didn't warn him we're moving. Just tell him you don't know anything about that. Tell him you're my cousin visiting from Scranton and that we were leaving as you arrived. Just act confused."

Bug couldn't help smiling at that. No one had to teach Chopsy how to act confused — he came by it naturally. "And there's a lot of food still in the cupboards," she added helpfully.

"You won't need it?" Chopsy asked. "I don't want to take food out of anyone's mouth."

"No, we got what we need," Walter assured him. "Take what you want."

"Thanks." Chopsy shook Walter's hand vigorously. "The country'll be good for both of you. I lived on a farm a while back. Drove a tractor. Picked fruit and vegetables. We grew strawberries that year. Oh, they was sweet. Pick one, eat one, all day long. That were one sweet job, my son."

As Chopsy chattered cheerfully on about strawberries, they left him to guard the truck and ran upstairs for one last look around to make sure they'd left nothing behind.

Driving Safely

It took less than five minutes for their final walk around
the apartment. As Bug trailed behind Walter, checking out
each corner and closet, she felt no connection to the nearly
empty rooms and abandoned furniture. It no longer felt like
home.

Yet she was sad, her eyes misty, her throat tight, as they
made their way down the dreary corridor to the stairs for the
last time. Walter was humming tunelessly again, one arm
wrapped lightly around Bug's shoulders, when old Mrs.
Klodsky opened her door just enough to stick her head out
and called: "You doing a flit, Walter? Landlord's not going to
be happy."

Walter laughed joyfully.

"You tell him we'll be back when we're rich. Then we're
gonna buy this building from him and fix it up proper.
Everyone will get a new fridge — and a free month's rent."

"I won't need any of it by then, Walter," she replied, readjusting her false teeth as she spoke. "I'm going to win the lottery soon, and when I do, I'm moving to the other side of the tracks."

"Right on, Mrs. Klodsky. We can't wait for that lottery of yours, though," Walter chuckled. "We're off to make our own luck. Starting today."

Bug wasn't very fond of Mrs. Klodsky because she was a nosy busybody who was always spying on the neighbors, peering out through a crack in her doorway or peeking through the blinds of her small kitchen window. Bug should be happy to be leaving Mrs. Klodsky behind in the dark little apartment building. And she had to admit that she wouldn't really miss much about the apartment at all, with its constant barrage of noise in the middle of the night — babies crying, televisions turned up too loud, the thump of stereos with too much bass — and the often unappetizing smell of other people's cooking that lingered for days in the dim hallways. It didn't really make sense to be sad about leaving, but ever since Walter's breakfast announcement, Bug had been feeling odd — bad, sad and mad. She didn't know exactly what she felt, but she knew it wasn't happy.

When they returned to the street, Chopsy was in the midst of chasing some kids away from the truck, and he looked relieved to see them.

"Glad you're back, Walter," he said breathlessly. "Those kids were trying to climb up and steal stuff out from under your tarp. I tried to stop them. Heck, I did stop them. I was worried your plan would be ruined if they got into your truck."

Bug was waiting for him to launch into a string of cuss words, but he caught himself in midsyllable and ended up just spluttering in frustration. Walter put up a hand to silence Chopsy and switched the conversation over to his new set of wheels.

"So what do you think of Safely?" he boomed. Both Bug and Chopsy looked at him blankly.

"Safely. The truck's name is Safely. You know, so that wherever we go, I'll always be driving Safely."

Chopsy almost fell down laughing, but Bug just grimaced. The truck's appearance did nothing to lift her spirits. Parked in front of a fire hydrant, Safely was an eyesore — old and junky-looking. It had certainly seen better days. It might have been red once, but it was now just a brownish, battered wreck, sporting one green fender and one blue, both salvaged from a scrapyard after the originals had rusted off.

Walter opened the driver's door, motioning for Bug to climb in first and slide across to the passenger side. Then he pulled himself up behind the steering wheel and put the key into the ignition. When he cranked the engine, it stuttered and sputtered and roared to life, faded for a second, then roared again.

Waving to Chopsy, Walter wrestled the truck into gear and eased Safely out onto Clancy Street. He tooted the horn twice and burst into song.

"Swing low, sweet chariot,

Coming for to carry us hommmme.

Swing low, sweeet char-i-o-ot . . ."

"Some chariot, eh, Bug? Don't you worry — this is gonna work out great. Nonstop excitement. Success guaranteed."

They had gone only about three blocks when Walter

pulled the rig over, grinding through the gears as he slowed, revving the engine in an attempt not to stall out. The din of the idling motor was numbing, and Bug was tempted to roll up her window despite the summer heat.

"I almost forgot my new boots," hollered Walter over the noise of the engine. He pulled out a pair of tooled leather cowboy boots from under the seat. "The guy at the warehouse gave these to me. Said I needed to dress like a trucker if I was going on the road."

He laughed as he wriggled his bare feet into the high-cut boots, then pushed his sandals under the seat. Bug had not met any truckers before, but she felt confident that Walter would not be mistaken for one so long as he stuck to wearing psychedelic T-shirts and oversized cargo shorts.

Testing his boots on the brake and clutch pedals, Walter roared his approval. "Much easier on the feet. I'll be able to drive all night," he announced to Bug, who smiled thinly. Hitting the turn signal, Walter lurched out into traffic, almost hitting an approaching minivan, which screeched to a halt to avoid an accident. Ignoring the blaring horn, Walter steered the truck back into his own lane and waved grandly, as if the driver had done him a favor. Then the Hapensaks, with all their worldly goods, bounced down Clancy Street toward the expressway.

On the Road

The nonstop excitement Walter promised began as soon as they turned onto the highway. Although it was unclear to Bug whether her father lacked highway driving skills or whether the truck was just severely underpowered, it quickly became apparent that the expressway was a mistake.

The truck grumbled and coughed its way up the entrance ramp but was unable to keep up with the flow of traffic. Relying on the truck's size rather than speed, Walter rumbled across two busy lanes of traffic while cars and trucks whizzed past on either side, some drivers blasting their horns and shaking their fists in anger.

"That's road rage," hooted Walter merrily. "These folks are rushing home or off to their cottages for the weekend, and they forget their manners. Look at them all charging mindlessly in the same direction. Like a bunch of gerbils. And for what? They'll just turn around and head back in two days."

Gerbils? Bug was tempted to explain to Walter that he actually meant lemmings but decided to do it another time. The windows were down, and the rush of the wind and the roar of the passing traffic — not to mention the racket of the truck and its wildly flapping tarpaulin — made thoughtful conversation impossible. She debated whether to tell him at the same time that lemmings did not, in fact, follow each other in droves over the edge of cliffs. It was a myth, but perhaps Walter would not be receptive to this information. He was stubborn and, on more than one occasion, had abandoned a meal for a quick trip to the library to check a fact that might prove him right.

* * *

Their time on the high-speed expressway was mercifully short. Within a few minutes, traffic slowed abruptly, brought to a snail's pace by an accident far off in the distance. Six lanes of traffic became hopelessly snarled. The smell of exhaust fumes was awful, and it was getting uncomfortably hot in the cab of the truck. And, to top it off, wisps of steam began to waft from under the truck's hood, a sign that Safely was starting to overheat.

"We gotta get out of here before the engine blows a hose," announced Walter. He signaled to make a right-lane change. "Is it clear?"

Bug looked down at two laughing women having an animated conversation in a saucy red sports car with its top down. Their happy chatter, however, turned to mute terror when they noticed the dump truck nosing into their lane.

"There's a little car beside us," warned Bug nervously.

"Oh, they'll let us in. Just wave and smile at them."

Bug gave an embarrassed finger waggle as the driver of the sports car struggled to steer clear of the sputtering truck. With a friendly tap on the horn, Walter eased through two more lanes of traffic, heading for an exit he had spotted just ahead on the right.

"Lucky that we're so big," he guffawed. "Safely is so old and ugly, no one is going to chance getting in our way. Keep waving, and let me know when we're clear."

* * *

Even after finding Route 2, it was another hour before they reached the outskirts of the city. Bug could have fallen asleep from heat and exhaustion if the ride had been smoother, but the heavy traffic and endless stoplights kept Walter busy shifting gears, and the truck jerked forward every time he let out the clutch.

But once she got used to the bouncing ride, Bug began to relax and look around, her feet propped up on the ancient chrome dashboard, her head rocking back and forth against the doorpost. There was no danger of falling out, as the door — missing the handle and armrest — had been welded shut years before.

"You've got to love a truck, eh?" thundered Walter over the loud whine of the engine. "You can see forever, and nobody gets in your way." She nodded silently and had to admit to herself that he was right. They had never owned a car that she could remember, always riding buses and subway trains to wherever they were going in the city. But now, all that was behind them, and they were free to go wherever they wanted.

26

Gazing down from her high perch, barely listening to Walter's nonstop commentary, Bug noted an endless string of shopping plazas, fast-food restaurants and boxy discount stores, each one surrounded by a sea of parked cars. She occasionally recognized the name of a store from a television ad or a radio jingle. Honest Mel's Used Cars. Fat Bucky's Carpets. Crazy Lionel's Discount Appliances.

"I went to school with that guy Lionel," Walter was saying when Bug tuned him back in. "He and his brother were so poor, they took turns wearing the same winter coat in grade four. Now look at him. Richer than stink. That'll be us in a few years' time, except we'll make a little less money and make a whole lot of people happy."

* * *

They pulled in at a burger joint for dinner. As they ate, Bug considered asking where they were going, but she suspected that Walter didn't know yet, so she kept silent, not wanting to encourage him to speculate out loud. As always, though, there was little chance of Walter's keeping quiet for long. He had obviously been thinking of a plan and was eager to share it with her.

"We're going to find a nice little town that hasn't been spoiled by all these big franchise stores and restaurants yet," he declared, emphasizing his point with a stab of a long, straight french fry. As he did, a bit of ketchup flipped off and sailed across the table.

"It's gotta be a place where there is still room for a little guy with a big idea. We'll know it when we see it, you watch. We'll sell our shoes, and maybe the truck, and use the money

27

to start something that people want, that they really need. Something no one else has thought of."

"Like what?" Bug asked, unable to contain herself. Walter's enthusiasm was starting to take hold of her too, as it usually did.

"I don't know yet, honey. But we'll know when we find the place. We'll pull in and look around and say, 'You know what this place needs is a . . .' And whatever it is, that's the business we'll go into."

"You make it sound easy," said Bug.

"Well, it may not be easy," he replied, scratching his beard thoughtfully, "but we'll do all right. We're a good team." He stood up and stretched his arms wide, then did a quick series of bends and back arches as if he were an athlete preparing for a marathon. While a few customers chuckled at his diner calisthenics, the waitress hurried over with their bill, anxious to move her eccentric customer along before he started a full aerobic workout.

"We've got a lot of miles ahead of us tonight, so let's hit the road," he declared, holding the door open for Bug.

Worms on the Side

The sun had been up for more than an hour when Walter Hapensak coaxed the decrepit dump truck into the parking lot of Betty's Burger 'N Bait diner. It was 7 o'clock on Saturday morning, August 28, and Walter was fairly bouncing with energy.

"Bug, wake up. Time for breakfast," he sang out, reaching down to nudge his sleeping daughter. He had driven all night while she had been curled up in a sleeping bag on the floor of the truck.

"What time is it?" she groaned. "I don't think I got a minute's sleep last night."

"Ahhh, you slept all right. Every so often, you'd call out and thrash around a bit, but you slept most of the night."

"Where are we?" As Bug spoke, she proceeded to untangle herself from the sleeping bag and blankets that had been her bed. Her legs had been tucked underneath the seat, and she had trouble sliding them out so that she could sit up. A broken seat spring caught a corner of the sleeping bag, and Bug gave a little kick to unsnag it, which in turn sent a couple of soda cans rolling across the floor.

"Place called Wamble. Never heard of it before, but it looks nice enough," Walter enthused. He was always much too energetic at this hour in the morning for Bug's taste. "Judging by all the trucks in the parking lot, I'd guess this is a sure bet for breakfast."

Bug had finally struggled up onto the seat and was twisting the rear-view mirror to the right to take a look at her hair.

"Uh-oh, hair alert," she declared. "Where's my brush?"

"I would guess it's in the back of the truck with everything else we own, Bug," said Walter. "You look fine. Just drag your fingers through your hair and tie that bandanna thing around your head. No one will notice."

He started to open his door and paused as it screeched on its ancient hinges. "We'll have a nice breakfast here, and then we'll make a plan — you'll see. Everything will work out fine."

Great, thought Bug, another Walter Hapensak plan is about to be unleashed on the unwitting citizens of . . .

"What did you say the name of this place is?" she asked her father.

"Wamble, as in let's wamble on in and get some breakfast."

. . . of Wamble, she thought. Look out, world, the Hapensaks have landed.

* * *

A dozen early-morning patrons at Betty's Burger 'N Bait

30

were vigorously arguing the merits of Florida retirement communities, but when the tinny bell over the door announced the arrival of the two strangers, all conversation stopped.

Betty, a tall, thin woman in her early sixties, had just declared that she intended to spend her final years knee-deep in salt water, fishing in the surf for anything big enough to mount on the wall, when she spotted her new customers.

Bug would have attracted little enough attention if she had been by herself, although some might have commented on her wiry frame or the fact that she looked as if she had just climbed out of bed after a bad night. But it was Walter who inspired the sudden silence and the bemused looks among Betty and her customers.

Over her 12 years with Walter, Bug had grown almost immune to his lack of fashion sense. When they were alone in the truck, she didn't give his outfit a second thought, but as soon as they entered the diner and everyone turned to stare, she recognized the look of amusement on their faces. She had seen it countless times before — on city streets, in shopping malls and grocery stores, at parent-teacher interviews.

Suddenly self-conscious at the attention, Bug stopped and tried to retreat, but her father, close behind, blocked her escape. He smiled broadly at Betty and her clientele, cavalierly swept his brimless, embroidered hat off his head and said hello in a cheery, spirited way.

While it was true enough that Betty's customers had all seen sheepskin vests, tie-dyed shirts, baggy cargo shorts and cowboy boots before, they had never seen all of them on one person at the same time.

The cowboy boots, thought Bug, glancing back at her father's spindly bare legs, are definitely a mistake.

But nothing ever deterred Walter Hapensak from striding into the midst of strangers and striking up a conversation. He kept right on going, steering Bug by the shoulders and nodding to everyone he passed. His cowboy boots slapped noisily against his bare calves as he angled across the room toward two empty stools at the counter.

"A coffee, please, double-sugar, double-cream, a large orange juice and a couple of menus," he called down the counter to Betty as he straddled one of the stools. Bug remained standing, wishing they had chosen a booth by the window, but her father was obviously planning to engage the locals in an entrepreneurial discussion and had planted himself in the center of the customers seated at the counter and the nearby tables.

Sensing the girl's hesitation to sit down next to a stranger, a droopy-faced dairy farmer named Orville Waters slipped away from the counter with his coffee in hand and joined two men at a table.

"Thanks," Bug mumbled as she sat down.

Orville nodded shyly as his friends chuckled at the old farmer's gallantry. Meanwhile, the drinks and menus had arrived. Bug seized her menu and buried her face in it, hoping that the men would turn their attention elsewhere. She quickly scanned the breakfast section, looking for something healthier to eat than greasy bacon, eggs dripping griddle fat and white-bread toast.

Walter sipped his coffee under Betty's watchful eyes,

contemplating his choices and doing a little quick math in his head.

"Have anything you like, Bug," he urged loudly enough for everyone to hear but added in a whisper, "just try to keep it under four bucks." Money was tight, and he hoped they could both eat a hearty breakfast for less than $10.

"What'll it be, folks?" asked Betty. She had moved closer and was now standing in front of Bug.

"I'll have the Fisherman's Special, with bacon, eggs over easy, home fries and white toast," said Walter decisively. "And my daughter here will have . . ." He looked at Bug expectantly.

"A bowl of oatmeal and a side order of toast. Whole wheat toast, please."

Betty paused, then turned to Walter and asked, "Will you be wanting worms with the special?"

"Worms?" Confused, Walter looked to Bug for help, but she just shrugged her shoulders. "Worms?" he repeated.

"Night crawlers," Betty answered.

Still baffled, Walter smiled helplessly, looking to Bug again for assistance. In response, she thrust her face deeper inside the menu, quickly scanning the list of side orders to see whether worms were a main course or an appetizer.

"Night crawlers? Those big, fat juicy ones? How do you serve them?" asked a perplexed Walter.

"In a little container with some peat moss to keep them moist. But you don't have to have them. You can get coffee instead."

Suddenly, Bug understood. "Oh . . . they're not for eating — they're for bait. Right here, it says half a dozen bait worms

33

free with every Fisherman's Special served before 8 o'clock."

The diner erupted into gales of laughter. Betty, with tears streaming down her cheeks, was laughing so hard she was bent over double. She laid one hand on Walter's shoulder and wheezed, "Jeez, mister, I'm sorry, but that always gets the tourists." She wiped the tears from her face with a corner of her apron, took a deep breath and continued, "You see, this place started out as a bait shop, and we put the worms on the menu years ago to keep the fishermen happy."

Walter laughed heartily along with the others and turned to Bug, hoping that the joke had improved her glum mood. But she had spotted the restroom sign in a distant corner of the diner and was headed there before he could say a word.

Pickerel

A New Plan

When she reached the twin doors of the restrooms, Bug looked up at the signs and shook her head. It seemed that nobody in these little diners was ever happy with simple MEN and WOMEN signs. Instead, they tried to be all cutesy with goofy pictures and corny gags.

Betty's signs had two cartoon fish leaping out of the water. One was curvaceous, with curly eyelashes and pouty lips; the other, leaner and longer, had chiseled pecs. The fish were labeled Pickerel and Pike. Choosing the pouty pickerel, Bug pushed the door open and entered.

As diner restrooms go, it was not bad, clean but not fancy, and Bug didn't hesitate to fill the washbasin with water to rinse her face. She still had sleep lines on one of her cheeks, and her fingers had the orange remnants of last night's bedtime bag of Cheezo-Puffs. The cold water was refreshing. She scooped up several double handfuls, bringing her face down into the dripping pools each time until she felt wide awake. Then, pumping some foamy pink soap from a dispenser, she gave her hands and fingers a good scrub and dried them under a noisy hot-air blower before pulling off the bandanna to examine her hair.

It certainly needed a wash, but she could survive another day. Bug pulled strands of hair through her fingers, wishing that she had kept out a brush or comb — and a toothbrush — when they had packed the previous day. But everything she owned was stuck in the back of Walter's old truck and out of reach until they got to where they were going.

Ha! Where were they going? That was the million-dollar question, and there was no ready answer.

Bug had seen her father hatch some pretty wild schemes over the years, but this unmatched-running-shoe business was the craziest by far. People who didn't know Walter could easily become caught up in his excitement and enthusiasm, and everyone agreed that he was a great salesman. Yet the sad truth was, he always seemed to be selling the wrong thing in the wrong place at the wrong time.

His kite business in City Park a few summers ago, for instance, had thrived for almost a month, until the city council passed a law banning kite flying on city property. So many people were flying Walter's kites that by the end of each day, the trees were littered with the tattered remnants of wrecked kites and the ground was covered in tangled kite string. Kite fliers, gazing skyward, were constantly running into one another, and two men had been arrested for fighting after their kites collided and crashed. When the fire department had to be dispatched three times in a single day to rescue people from trees they had climbed to retrieve their kites, the city council decided to issue its ban.

When Walter switched to boomerangs and Frisbees, the city extended its "aerial recreation" ban to include the throwing of anything other than a ball and proceeded to add model-rockets and remote-controlled airplanes just in case Walter branched into other fields of amateur aeronautics. By the end of that summer, Walter had been reduced to selling yo-yos and bouncy rubber balls, and all his customers had to sign a legal document promising not to sue the city if they were injured while playing with them in the park.

The thought of what might go wrong with unmatched running shoes was almost too much for Bug to bear. If they lost all their money on this venture, they would be in big trouble. They had given up their apartment, abandoned half their furniture and left the only city she had ever known. If the shoe business flopped, they would be as homeless as Chopsy. Closing her eyes, she shuddered as she imagined what it would be like having to live under the Flatsview Bridge with the ragged, grubby old men who sought shelter there.

Back to Reality

Staring blankly into the bathroom mirror at Betty's Burger 'N Bait, Bug was startled out of her reverie by a gentle knock at the door. Embarrassed, she called, "Just a minute" and reached over to flush the toilet, then ran some water noisily into the sink so that whoever was waiting outside the door would think she had been doing something other than merely daydreaming.

Opening the Pickerel door, Bug came face-to-face with a smiling but concerned Betty. "Didn't want to rush you, darlin', but I think your daddy's getting a bit worried because you've been gone so long. I just thought I'd check on you. You OK? You're not sick or nothing, are you?"

Bug shook her head, her cheeks blushing red.

"Now don't go getting all shy on me there," Betty cooed. "We girls have the right to spend as much time getting gussied up as we want. Men were born to wait for us —

fathers and husbands. Now you go on out there and eat your breakfast. From what old Wally has been telling us, you've had a long, hard night."

Wally? Bug had never heard anyone call her father Wally before. And what on earth had he been telling them?

In the restaurant, Walter was the focus of attention. Leaning back against the counter, he sat astride the red and chrome stool as if it were a horse and fidgeted it back and forth. His breakfast plate was almost empty, and he held his coffee cup in one hand as he spoke, waving a fork in the air to emphasize his points.

Hearing Bug approach, he smiled broadly. "Fellows, this is my daughter Bug. She's the administrative brains of the operation. I've got the instinct to spot an opportunity a mile away, and she has the good sense to keep me organized."

Bug smiled briefly and sat down in front of her breakfast while the men all mumbled their greetings.

"I can warm up that cereal for you, darlin'," called Betty, who had hustled back behind the counter and was getting ready to top off everyone's coffee.

Bug shook her head slightly and added a packet of brown sugar to the oatmeal, keeping her eyes down.

Walter turned back to the coffee drinkers, who were all listening with rapt attention to what he was saying.

"So, as I was telling you, we've got a truckload of really good sports shoes — odds and sods but all brand-new and top quality — and we need a place to sell them."

The group all nodded thoughtfully in agreement while Betty picked up the coffee pot and made her way through the tables and chairs, filling coffee cups and removing dirty dishes as she went.

"So you're looking for a store or something for a week or so, right?" said one of the locals.

"Nope. Don't need anything that fancy," Walter replied. "Just clear weather and a dry spot where people gather."

"The old hardware store down on King Street is empty," suggested an old man seated by the cash register.

"He doesn't want a store," the man sitting next to him said loudly. "He wants someplace free. Outside."

"Nothing's free anymore," snorted the old man, fumbling with his hearing aid. "My batteries are dead again. Need new ones. Even have to pay to hear these days."

The conversation was threatening to turn into a discussion about hearing aids or high prices, and Walter struggled to bring them back to his problem.

"You must have a farmer's market or something around here on Saturday," he said, "where people rent space and sell produce."

"Nearest one of those today is in Amaranth, about an hour's drive east," declared a slight man wearing a yellow John Deere cap. "All kinds of people sell things there. Day like today, it'll be packed with city folks looking for fresh corn and such."

"City folks can't seem to buy the stuff up fast enough," said his table companion. "And they love haggling over prices to get a good deal. My son-in-law goes there every week with anything he can load on his truck, and he comes home at the end of the day with his pockets full of money."

Walter slapped his hand on the counter gleefully. "Hear that, Bug? Now that sounds like just the ticket."

Before Bug could answer, Orville Waters, the dairy farmer, interrupted.

"Can't do it. They make you pay for the full season. Besides, there hasn't been an empty spot all summer. You show up uninvited, the manager will call the cops. You'd be better off doing it here in Wamble — down at the old market square in front of the town hall. It's open every Wednesday and Saturday. Cost you $10 for the day, and every soul in town drops by for a peek."

"Even better," Walter crowed. "Where is it?"

"Just down the road a piece. But you can't set up there today."

"No?"

"Nope. The Tichburg Harvest Fair's on. Won't be anybody selling or buying at the Wamble market today. They might as well just shut this whole town down on fair day. Heck, half the businesses along King Street will likely be closed by noon, so's fellas can take their families out to the fair."

Bug had finished her oatmeal and was working on her toast, eating around the crust, which had gone rock-hard as it cooled. "So, Walter, why don't we just go to the fair if that's where everyone is?"

Before Walter could reply that he'd been thinking the exact same thing, the diner erupted with hoots and guffaws. Orville was laughing so hard that coffee shot out his nose, and he started choking and coughing, while the deaf old man near the cash register kept asking what was so darn funny.

Bug glared around at the bunch of them, assuming that

41

they were making fun of her until Betty bent over the counter behind her and said, "Pay no mind to these old boys, dearie. They're not laughing at you. At least, not directly. It's just the thought of your daddy there pulling up at the gates to the Harvest Fair in Tichburg and explaining to Doc Timmerman that he wants to . . ."

" . . . sell a dump truck load of lost running shoes," one of the men interjected.

"Well," Betty added, "it's just a funny picture, darlin', that's all."

A Plan Takes Shape

Five minutes after hearing about the Tichburg Harvest Fair, Walter Hapensak had formulated a plan that he was sure would change their lives forever.

"Forever?" Bug sighed as they walked across the parking lot toward Safely. "Walter, do we have to start changing things forever right away? Can't we just start with someplace to sleep tonight?"

But once Walter was on a roll, there was no way to dampen his enthusiasm. They would drive out to the fairground, he explained, somehow get past Doc Timmerman (who, Betty had explained, ran the show and could be a very difficult man to deal with), dump their shoes into a huge pile and sell them for $5 apiece. He figured they would need to sell only 400 shoes to earn enough to live on for the next two to three months. If they sold more, they would be set up for a long time — maybe the whole winter.

It was almost 8 o'clock, and the sun was starting to warm the pavement. Across the road, a few cars and pickup trucks were parked at a building-supply store, but traffic was still sparse. Next door at a service station, a loud DING announced the arrival of a customer at the gas pumps, and as Bug glanced over, she saw a sloppy-looking teenage boy in a bright red shirt and long, baggy black shorts shuffle over to the car.

The road toward the downtown section of Wamble was lined by a string of big, old brick houses, many of which had been converted into businesses — an insurance office, a funeral home, an antique shop. Looking down Route 2, Walter and Bug could see a jumble of signs amid the tall, leafy trees that bordered the sidewalk.

"Tell me what you see, Bug," Walter said.

"Bunch of old houses. Lots of trees."

"Well, that's right. Now tell me what you don't see."

Bug pondered the challenge. "I don't see anyone selling lemonade at the end of a driveway. Or worms. Or shoes."

Walter laughed and hugged his daughter. "That's true. But I don't see any Golden Arches either. No big electric signs for Burger Barn or Whacko-Taco or Crazy Lionel's or any factory outlets. Bug, I feel like Christopher Columbus discovering a new land. There's opportunity for us here."

"Well, just don't forget about the natives," Bug quipped as she climbed up into the truck. "They might not all be as friendly as Betty."

"Don't you worry. They're going to love us — and our shoes."

* * *

Breakfast had come to less than $8 with the tip, and when Betty had handed Walter his change, Bug had scooped up $2 and convinced Walter to buy a Scratch-a-Lotta lottery ticket — top prize a million dollars. Now in the truck, she was itching to start scratching.

"Let's just rub off those little spots right now," she had pleaded as Walter started the engine. "If we win, then we can forget everything else. Get a fantastic car — maybe a convertible — and keep on driving."

But Walter had tucked the lottery ticket into his massive wallet, and there it would stay.

"We don't need that ticket today," he explained. "We've got a different kind of luck working for us, the kind you have to earn by being smart and trying something new."

"Please let me scratch it," Bug begged.

"Maybe tomorrow. If you try it today and we win, we'll never know whether we could have done it by ourselves. And if we lose, well, then it might just jinx the whole shoe sale. We'll set it aside for a rainy day, when we really need some good luck."

* * *

Walter pulled in to the service station to get some gas. Up close, the young gas jockey was a round-faced pimply kid with dark, greasy hair. While the teenager pumped gasoline into the tank, Walter stood to one side making conversation with him.

"Will there be many people at the Tichburg fair, you think?"

"Oh, yeah. Everybody from around here. I'll be there soon myself. Just have to work another hour. Costs a lot to keep a

45

high-performance car on the road, so's I work overnight shifts almost every weekend." He directed Walter's attention to an old black Camaro parked in one of the station's service bays, its hood up and its stereo pumping out a throbbing rap beat. "Mind you, it's worth it. People pay attention when you got good wheels. Me, I cruise all week and work weekends to pay for it."

He paused and assessed the truck he was serving and smirked. "So whatcha hauling today? Garbage? Dump's more or less on the way to the fairground, I guess. Just don't turn this old bomb off while you're there, or someone might mistake it for scrap."

As Bug listened to the teen, her "jerk alarm" went off.

Walter ignored the kid's lame joke. "A truckload of shoes, actually," he replied. "We're set up for a big sale of sports shoes at the fair. Got a really good deal on brand-new running shoes. You run much?"

"Man, I don't even walk much. When you got wheels like I do, you don't hafta use your feet. Except for accelerating and braking — and I don't do a lotta braking."

Bug slouched lower in her seat, afraid that her father would launch into a detailed description of their bizarre shoe business. She was starting to get a sense of just how awful this whole shoe thing was going to be. Oh, well, she thought, at least nobody knew her in this part of the world.

Country Roads

Bug watched as Walter carefully counted out $75 for their fuel and realized that it must have cost a fortune to get this far on their trip. Although she had no idea how much money they had when they started, she knew that it couldn't have been much. But Walter didn't seem worried as he climbed back into the cab.

"Next stop, Tichburg," he roared above the rumbling engine, then burst into a tuneless song: "We're off to see the wizard, the wonderful wizard of Tich."

They followed the highway through the center of Wamble, a quiet little town that boasted three sets of traffic signals along its main street. Most of the stores looked as though they were from another time, and Bug squinted her eyes half shut trying to imagine everything in black and white, as if she were in an old television show.

"Hey, I think I just saw the Beaver playing with Opie," she

47

shouted to Walter, dredging up the only names she could remember from the vintage TV shows they sometimes watched together on Saturday mornings. But Walter couldn't hear what she said over the roar of the truck and simply responded to the upbeat tone of her voice, thinking, no doubt, that she was enthusiastic about the charms of Wamble.

"Darn right."

The final block of stores (a dress shop, butcher shop, bakery and two banks) gave way to a small, shady park with benches and a drinking fountain. Next to the open green space of the park stood a library with huge columns and an imposing front stairway, and beside that was an even larger church. A couple of elderly ladies wearing big straw hats were chatting on the church steps, each with a little dog on a leash. Walter honked his horn and waved, inspiring them to wave hesitantly at the smiling stranger driving by.

"Friendly folks, that's for sure," he chortled as he shifted gears. The downtown area had quickly given way to a couple of blocks of big Victorian houses set well back from the sidewalk, then to smaller homes, interrupted by a used-car lot and a tired-looking, run-down motel. Just ahead was a bridge, but before they got to it, Walter spotted the sign for Tichburg and swung right, onto a paved road that took them into the country.

Within minutes, they were in a river valley, driving past fields of tall corn and pastures with small herds of black and white cows grazing. As they passed a barnyard set close to the road, the smell of manure hit them both at the same time.

"Smell that sweet country air," boomed Walter teasingly, and Bug had to laugh. Just then, a huge black and brown dog

48

tore out from behind the barn and charged toward Bug's side of the truck, barking frantically. Bug worried that it was going to run right under the wheels of the truck, but it seemed to know how close it could get without being hit. It kept pace with them for a minute or so and then eased off, slowing to a trot. As they sped away, Bug watched the dog in the big side mirror as it jumped across a shallow ditch and trotted back home along the fence line, happy in the knowledge that it had driven off yet another intruder.

By this time, the road had pulled away from the river, heading uphill a bit, striking a route halfway between the river on the left and the top of a ridge that rose to the right. Looking down across the river, Bug could see more farms on the other side of the valley and a distant road running parallel to the one they were on. The sky was a rich azure blue flecked with white popcorn clouds, and the fields were a patchwork of greens and yellows, broken by trees and houses and barns. Despite her foreboding about Walter and his big adventure, Bug thought this was about the prettiest place she had ever seen. Pretty and quiet.

A few minutes farther along, they passed a large faded sign that read: Welcome to Tichburg. Population 473. Someone had tried to turn the "3" into a silhouette of a fat person, while another had scrawled "JL loves FA."

Soon they were passing houses surrounded by large expanses of carefully trimmed grass, and pulled up to an intersection with a flashing red light and a stop sign. There was a gas station on one corner, a dilapidated barn on another and large, old brick houses on the remaining two. A second road branched off the main road and led down a steep hill into the village itself.

Walter signaled left, shifted into low gear and started slowly down the slope, the truck straining against the gravity that was pulling it toward Tichburg. Across the road, a long, narrow banner announced: Annual Harvest Fair, August 27th and 28th.

"Well, Bug, we made it this far," yelled Walter over the whine of the creeping truck. "Are you ready to sell some shoes?"

Bug's initial reply was a silent shake of her head, but then she reconsidered and simply shrugged her shoulders, flashing her father a tentative smile.

"That's the spirit, sweetheart," Walter said, giving her a quick thumbs-up as he wrestled to keep the steering wheel under control.

Running Hot

It was easy to find the fairground. They simply followed the steady stream of pickup trucks and cars that turned at the fire station onto a wide street which led to the fairground gates. Their slow descent down the main-street hill had caused a small backup of traffic, and every one of the vehicles following them made the same turn.

Thin columns of steam were starting to rise up from under Safely's hood. "She's running hot. I think we're gonna be stopping over at the fair whether they want us to or not," said Walter, pointing at the temperature gauge on the dashboard. The needle was quivering in the red danger zone.

The entrance to the fairground was little more than two dirt tire tracks with a strip of grass growing down the middle. The lane passed beneath an ancient wooden archway whose blistered white letters read *ICHBURG FAIRGROUND*. The "T" was missing, and the "F" was dangling at a precarious angle. Bug wondered what would happen when the "F" finally fell to the ground. It would probably become a coveted prize hanging on some kid's bedroom wall.

The truck stuttered forward to a group of four men standing to one side of the gate. They wore small canvas aprons with pockets that bulged with money and tickets. Walter eased Safely ahead as the car in front of him passed through the gate, but when he pulled even with the men and braked to a stop, the truck's engine shuddered, sputtered and died. More thin ribbons of steam rose from beneath the hood.

Unfazed by the stalled engine, Walter leaned out of his window and greeted the men enthusiastically.

"Good day, fellows. We want to conduct a little business at your fair today. Where can we set up?"

The youngest of the men had hustled forward expecting to sell an admission ticket. He paused momentarily, glancing uncertainly back at his friends. Then he pointed to a tall man wearing a cowboy hat and sunglasses, who was standing in the back of a glistening white antique pickup truck scanning the fairground with binoculars, and said, "Doc Timmerman's the man to ask."

Turning to Bug, Walter smiled gleefully. "Wish me luck. I'm about to meet the Doc." He swung the creaking door open and jumped to the ground, scampering the short distance over to the man in the white truck.

Here it comes, thought Bug. We'll be run out of this place in two minutes flat. She was unsure how people were run out of small towns these days. In the old movies they watched on television, people were chased out of town in any number of ways, sometimes covered in tar and feathers, other times tied to poles and carried to the edge of the city limits. The flickering images in her head did little to calm her.

She watched the four admissions men laughing amongst themselves, no doubt over Walter's unusual fashion statement. The cowboy boots were all right with this crowd, but he really should have worn long pants.

Just before he stopped in front of Doc's pickup, Walter waggled his fingers at Bug in the salute he had been giving her since she was a baby. She waggled back at him, then turned away, afraid to watch what was about to unfold. She decided to look over the rest of the fairground from the safety of the truck cab.

Along the path, a short distance ahead, sprawled a dusty racetrack. Several vehicles had pulled onto the track, while others had crossed over to find parking spaces amongst the trees on the infield. Some had turned right, heading across a freshly cut hayfield toward half a dozen rows of parked cars. There were cars and pickup trucks everywhere. The entry road was choked with traffic, and there seemed no route out for anyone denied entrance.

Bug looked back toward Walter again and saw a boy about her age, maybe a bit younger, standing close to her father and listening intently to the discussion. Walter was clearly in full sell mode, gesturing dramatically and talking nonstop, but the tall man in the cowboy hat seemed unimpressed, shaking his head solemnly as he listened. The boy glanced her way, and she quickly scrunched down in her seat, hoping he didn't see her.

But Walter was not about to let her remain inconspicuous. Waving to catch her attention, he hollered over to ask how many RetroTred Hoopsters they had in the truck. Hoopsters, in Bug's opinion, were dopey — hideously huge basketball shoes that were, nonetheless, a hot commodity at school.

We're not even inside the gates, and he's already selling shoes to that kid, she thought. She had no idea how many Hoopsters were in the back, but she decided to be helpful when Walter threw out some numbers: 20? 30?

"Yeah," she answered loudly, rising in her seat. "At least 30." Then, to help clinch the sale, she asked, "What size?" She didn't catch the boy's reply but nodded to him, and his smile made it clear that he was excited by the prospect of buying unmatched running shoes. Everyone within earshot, from the Doc and the kid to the ticket sellers, was now looking her way, which made her feel shy again. Once more, she slumped down into the seat, hoping they would look elsewhere.

Within minutes, Walter was scrambling back into the cab, grinning as he coaxed the old truck to life. The engine caught, and he drove toward the men at the gate. "We're supposed to pay 50 bucks, but we'll have to pay on our way out — suffering a bit of a cash-flow crisis right now." He waved, and the men motioned him through the gate, indicating that he should turn right onto the track.

Bug looked back through the side-view mirror, expecting to see everyone rolling on the ground laughing, but the men had turned their attention to the long line of cars, and the cowboy-hat guy in the white truck had his binoculars glued to his eyes again. The kid had disappeared.

Underwear Exposed

Walter was absolutely ecstatic as he steered Safely along the dirt racetrack. He kept smiling over at Bug and, at one point, burst into another tuneless rendition of "Follow the Yellow Brick Road." As the last note died out, he explained that they were going to set up next to a hog-feed-company display, just up ahead on the left.

On their right was a small midway boasting about a dozen rides. Most of them were for little kids, but there were two Spin-Til-You-Barf rides and a Ferris wheel that was already in motion. Its buckets were empty, and two scruffy men were craning their necks as each one swept past, examining the undercarriages of the seats. Bug was about to remark on the puny midway, when her father spotted their space.

"That's where we're supposed to go. Up there on the left, just past the ball diamond." He steered toward several troughs and metal tanks that were being assembled by a couple of middle-aged men in jeans and matching golf shirts. They looked up in bewilderment as Walter turned the ramshackle truck toward them, waving enthusiastically as he cranked the steering wheel to the left.

There was barely enough room to squeeze Safely in between a tall, wooden utility pole that held lights for the ballpark and the neighboring pile of hog troughs, but he made it — almost without incident. Concentrating, as he was, on the hog display, he neglected to watch his side of the truck until he and Bug heard the sickening crunch of the driver's side mirror clipping the pole. They turned just in time to see the metal struts of the mirror snap, dropping the large mirror noisily onto the truck's running board.

The pole swayed slightly, and Bug was mortified, waiting for it to come crashing down on the truck and imagining that everyone was staring at them as Walter gunned the engine to ease farther forward. But as they climbed out the driver's door, no one seemed to have noticed the mishap. Walter immediately headed over to introduce himself to their fellow exhibitors, leaving Bug to clean up the broken mirror, which had fallen to the ground and been crushed by the big wheels of the truck. It was a hopeless mess, and Bug had just decided to abandon the task when Walter returned, all smiles and good cheer.

"What a terrific location," he said. "This is perfect — right across the track from the grandstand, where all the folks sit to watch the competitions. The only restrooms at the fairground are just over there, and every ballplayer at today's tournament has to walk right past us to get to the ball diamond. There isn't going to be a single person at the fair who won't notice us."

"Sounds perfect, all right," replied Bug. "We get to spend the whole day between a concrete outhouse and the world's newest hog-feed system, dodging foul balls while we sell unmatched running shoes to everyone in ICHBURG."

Walter ignored his daughter's sarcasm. "Turns out the guys next to us spend the whole summer traveling around to these little fairs demonstrating their equipment. They say folks aren't afraid to spend a lot of money when something catches their eye."

He had busied himself pacing the site and eyeing the patch of ground directly behind the truck, planning the best way to unload the shoes. Climbing atop one of the rear wheels, he loosened the ropes on one side of the tarp, then did the same on the other side. Warning Bug to stand clear and to keep curious onlookers well back, he stepped up into the cab, started the truck's engine and pulled the lever that would raise the dumper, then jumped out of the truck and walked over to join his daughter. The back of the truck rose slowly, creaking in protest, while everyone around them stopped to see what would come pouring out of the truck.

A few running shoes trickled out first, then Bug caught sight of their mattresses sliding off the top of the load. Within seconds, a flood tide of colorful shoes — no two alike — followed, completely burying the mattresses. The bucket was still rising higher. Walter had just started to laugh about the mattresses when he noticed a cardboard box come tumbling out, slowly at first, then in a rush.

"Oh, no, our stuff," he howled, tearing off for the cab in a hopeless attempt to stop the dumper, but it was too late.

Bug was frozen in place by the realization that all their worldly goods were about to go on display in the middle of a fairground filled with an ever-growing crowd of strangers. Two boxes of dishes and pots made a cacophonous noise as they crashed into each other before being crushed by a carton of books. This was quickly followed by a landslide of boxes amid an avalanche of shoes. Last to be spewed onto the ground were the stereo components and the TV, which rolled in slow motion down the mountain of shoes to land at Bug's feet.

Miraculously, only two of the boxes split open, spilling out an odd assortment of clothing and other personal items. As passersby turned to stare, Walter threw the lever to lower the dumper, then hustled back to assess the damage.

The most obvious casualty was the television set, which had a huge crack across its screen. But when Walter saw an array of his well-worn boxer shorts strewn the length of the shoe pile, he knew that Bug was probably suffering extreme embarrassment.

Seemingly rooted to the ground, Bug was horrified at the spectacle and did not move as Walter leaned over and gave her a comforting bear hug.

Smiling at the pig-trough guys who were approaching to offer to help clean up the mess, Walter rocked her gently back and forth. "Don't you worry. Things are going to be fine," he soothed. "Everyone is too busy setting up to even notice this mess. Besides, I was wondering which of those boxes had my clean underwear. And look. There's your hairbrush."

The Sales Pitch

It didn't take long to lift the boxes back into the truck. Bug gently carried the stereo and three armloads of clothing from the broken boxes to the cab for safekeeping but left the television on the ground beside the truck. The pig-guys had assured Walter that if he left it in plain view, someone would be sure to come by and offer to purchase it. Farmers, they claimed, didn't let anything go to waste.

"Some kid will steal it, more likely," Bug predicted, but Walter laughed, declaring that that would be all right too — if it were stolen, they wouldn't have to take it to the dump.

"It's not easy to get rid of something that big these days, Bug," he said optimistically. "I'll just be happy to see it gone one way or another. Can't really use a TV when you're on the road anyway."

Bug turned her attention to the mountain of shoes. It was an impressive pile, made even higher because it was resting

59

on top of the two mattresses. As they had fallen from the truck, the shoes had cascaded around the light standard and spread across the ground like a spilled package of gigantic colored candies. It was Bug's first clear view of the inventory, and she idly wandered around the edges, kicking errant shoes back onto the pile.

"So what do you think?" Walter was hovering at her elbow as he often did when he wanted her blessing for one of his half-baked money-making schemes.

"There's sure a lot of them."

"Good variety, though, right? Lots of colors and styles."

"I'll say. Probably too many if someone is looking for a match."

"Oh, I think it'll work out fine." Walter bent over and picked up a green high-top basketball shoe. "That kid over at the entry gate said he was looking for a pair of RetroTred Hoopsters — size seven. Let's figure he's a typical customer here. We'll get 'em started by helping them find one shoe that's going to fit, then we'll just sit back and let them pick through the pile to find another one.

"It's like fishing. The pile is the bait, and the first shoe they find is the hook. Once they're hooked, they'll stay here for hours looking for a matching, I mean, second shoe. Then we'll reel them in and take their money."

"So no one can find a perfect pair in here? Anywhere?" Bug asked.

"No, and we have to tell 'em that up front. You don't want a crowd of people thinking they've been cheated. But you say it to them in a way that they want to prove you wrong. Then they'll wade into the pile — waist-deep, if need be — and hunt until they find something they like, just to show you how smart they are. The longer they hunt, the more shoes they'll buy. The trick is to let *them* do the hunting. Then it'll be harder for them to give up. If *we* do the work, they'll just get bored and walk away without buying anything."

As he spoke, Walter was picking up shoes, checking their sizes and tossing them back. He continued holding on to the green Hoopster.

"We seem to have a lot of green left Hoopsters, mostly size sevens and tens."

"What about a red one?" Bug suggested. She slipped closer to the edge of the pile, picked one up and checked the size. "Seven. And it's a rightie."

"Congratulations, girl, you've just found the first salable pair. Set them aside in that busted box over there." He pointed to a box that had earlier held the contents of his sock and underwear drawer. "I suspect that one of our first customers is going to be that young fella we saw at the gate. And when he gives us his $10, he's going to be thinking how he just saved 100 bucks, not that he just blew his allowance on two mismatched shoes that we got for free."

At first, Bug considered arranging the shoes into some sort of order — perhaps by style or size — but Walter quickly dismissed the idea, explaining that that would take all the fun out of the hunt.

"Look at the fishpond over there on the midway. If people wanted organization and convenience, they'd just take their kids to the nearest Big Bang for Your Buck store and buy

61

them something. But they'd rather play the game, because they're not thinking about winning a cheap plastic toy — they're dreaming of catching something valuable.

"As for us, well, we're not selling shoes. We're selling an adventure."

It was never worth arguing with Walter at the best of times, so Bug accepted the advice easily, happy that she didn't have to do any extra work. For his part, Walter decided that they needed to put a sign on the pole that now rose out of the middle of the shoe pile. As they didn't have any markers or cardboard, he went off to scrounge up some materials.

"Just sit tight. I'll be right back. Anybody comes along, feel free to sell some shoes. But," and he paused meaningfully, "no free samples. We're selling shoes, not giving them away."

* * *

Finding nowhere else to sit, Bug gingerly climbed the pile of shoes and made a shallow nest near the top. Fidgeting and wiggling, she got as comfortable as possible, then began to look around at the preparations for the fair.

To her left, exhibitors were setting up tables and plastic lawn chairs in front of displays of farm equipment. Several huge tractors were parked beside the pig-guys, and past them, there were a couple of pickup trucks and some large pieces of agricultural equipment that Bug didn't recognize. They were all crammed inside one corner of the track's infield. Behind her, there was a corral where two teenage girls with long blonde hair tied back in ponytails rode horses around barrels spread about the enclosure, stopping occasionally to call out suggestions to a couple of men, who would then nudge one of the barrels a foot or two. A sign along the rail fence announced the annual District Barrel-Racing Championship.

Turning to her right, Bug saw a half-dozen other teenagers working on the baseball diamond, setting out bases, marking the baselines with white chalk and raking the dirt around home plate. A few players were tossing a ball back and forth in the outfield, while their coaches hunched forward on the team bench sipping coffee.

A grove of maple and oak trees rose up just beyond the ballpark, and Bug could see a collection of horse trailers and cars parked in the shady spots between the trees. Traffic into the fairground had picked up considerably, and vehicles that didn't cross the track into the trees either drove slowly along the track or cut across the distant field that separated the main gate from the grandstand.

The faded old wooden grandstand was perched atop a small hill directly across from where Bug sat, and she watched as people parked their cars in the field around it, then wandered off in all directions. There was a petting zoo to the left, with a midway, some tents and a few low buildings to the right. Sitting alone, nestled in her pile of shoes, Bug felt left out of the activities, even though she was in the middle of everything. It was like watching a colony of ants, she thought. They're all hustling and bustling, but only they know what's going on.

An antique fire truck with an open driver's seat and skinny little tires chugged along the track, passing by the display area and heading in the same direction that a dozen other vintage trucks and cars had gone in the past half hour. As it rounded the curve near the tractor exhibit, the fire truck backfired, issuing a huge bang that didn't seem possible for such a small vehicle. The noise startled the livestock across the track, and the barrel-racing horses behind Bug snorted nervously.

Peering across the track in search of Walter, Bug realized she had no idea which way he had gone. With his classic embroidered hat, though, he should not be hard to pick out in this crowd, where most of the men were wearing ball caps or Stetsons, but she could see no sign of him.

She did spot the boy who had told Walter he wanted a pair of Hoopsters when they were checking in. He was on a bicycle — the kind with the high handlebars and small wheels — and at first, she thought he was coming her way. But after coasting down the hill toward her, he turned onto the track and pedaled furiously, seemingly intent on catching up to the fire truck.

As she watched, a brown and white beagle dashed in front of the bike. The boy swerved, lost control and crashed to the ground, letting go of the handlebars as he rolled across the dirt. He didn't seem hurt and jumped quickly to his feet.

Bug craned her neck for a better look and, surprising herself, called out to the kid, who had bent over to pick up his bicycle. "Hey, you . . . what's-yer-name."

The boy dusted the dirt from his khaki pants before heading toward her. "Frogger," he yelled.

What a strange thing to say, thought Bug. She hesitated. Frogger? Was it a secret greeting? Curious, she slid down from her perch and watched as he approached.

First Impressions

"What?" she said abruptly. She realized her response may have sounded rude, but it was too late now.

The boy came nearer. He stopped within an arm's length of Bug and said, "Frogger" once more.

She frowned and gave him a puzzled look.

"You asked what my name was," he explained.

Bewildered, Bug wondered what he was talking about. She hadn't asked any such thing.

"No, I didn't," she said, shaking her head.

The boy looked at Bug curiously. "You yelled, 'What's your name?' And I told you. Frogger."

Bug paused for a second to remember her exact words and then replied, "No. I called you 'what's-yer-name' because I didn't know what your name was."

"Oh," said Frogger, nodding.

Now Bug was beginning to feel a bit stupid. Why on earth

had she called out to him? Kids fell off their bicycles every day, and she didn't make it a practice to talk to them. She smiled at him uncertainly and plowed ahead with her end of this somewhat awkward conversation.

"What kind of name is Frogger, anyway?"

She knew that it really wasn't any of her business and that she was giving him a hard time, yet he remained pleasant. He actually seemed to be a nice kid.

"Frogger's just a nickname," he answered. "My real name is Thaddeus — Thaddeus Archibald. They used to call me Tad, until I got to kindergarten. Then they called me Tadpole, and when I grew older, they started calling me Frogger. So what's your name?"

The question caught Bug off guard. She paused to consider her response. Having made fun of his name, it would be foolhardy to tell him her name was Bug. And she didn't want to introduce herself as Belinda Hapensak, which was her real name. Belinda Viola Hapensak. She thought about making up a name on the spot. If this was her new life starting today, why not invent another name to go with it? It wasn't likely they would be sticking around here anyway. Would she ever see this kid again?

But then she thought she'd just change the subject. She looked around for a distraction.

Staring past Frogger toward the grandstand, Bug scanned the knots of people in search of Walter again. If she saw him, she could put a quick end to this conversation, but luck was not on her side. Or was it? As she was looking around, she spotted something pink on the racetrack where Frogger

66

had crashed his bicycle. She pointed to it. "Is that yours?"

Bug started walking quickly toward the track, looking in both directions for oncoming traffic or livestock. "There's something over there where you dumped your bike."

Frogger dropped his bicycle to the ground at the edge of the pile of shoes and raced over to the track, but Bug beat him to it, almost stepping in a cow pie on her way. Yuck! Gross, she thought.

She picked up the object and examined it. It was small and pink. Very pink. A shocking hot pink. Once, when she was eight, Walter had given her some Barbie dolls and accessories, and this reminded her of all that awful bright pink junk that had lain in the back of her closet for almost two years before she sold it at a yard sale between moves.

Frogger reached for the object, but Bug pulled it back — not to be mean but . . . well . . . just to tease him a bit.

"Don't tell me," she joked. "It's your Barbie walkie-talkie." As she uttered these words, she realized that what she held was actually a pager. Some of the kids at school had had them. They had thought they were so cool, but in fact, most of their messages had come from their parents checking up on them, wanting to know where they were and when they'd be home. This kid must have real problems if his parents had given him a hot-pink pager. Maybe they had always wanted a daughter — a Froggette.

"It's a pager. I'm a firefighter, and that's my pager."

A firefighter!? Why do kids, especially boys, have to tell such ridiculous, exaggerated stories? Bug couldn't let this one go unchallenged.

67

"A firefighter?" She looked at him. He was normal enough looking, maybe even cute. But he was shorter than she was. "A midget firefighter?"

Had she really said that out loud? Too late to take it back now. As Walter would say, you can't put the toothpaste back in the tube. So she continued talking.

"This is really weird. When we pulled off the highway and found this place, I told my dad that it felt totally weird, but this is way beyond weird."

Bug was on a roll and kept going. Talking without thinking.

"Are your fire trucks pink too?" she teased.

"No. Red and yellow."

She tried to smile. Laugh a bit. The way she did when poking fun at Walter. But it came out all wrong.

"Like red with yellow stripes or yellow with red polka dots?" Polka dots? Bug wondered where that had come from. It sounded so dumb. She was acting like a first-class jerk, and she hated jerks.

But Frogger didn't seem to mind. He wasn't mad or anything. He just launched into an explanation about the different kinds of fire trucks they had and where they had got them. She interrupted him.

"You mean you really are a firefighter? How old are you?"

He said he was 12. Well, nearly 12. Almost the same age as me, she thought. And then he told Bug he was a special assistant to the area's fire chief. A woman fire chief. That got Bug's attention.

"A woman fire chief. That's cool. So she's just really into pink, huh?"

68

"No," replied Frogger. "It was the only color available at the store." Bug could sympathize with that, glancing over at the huge pile of unmatched running shoes she and Walter were about to sell to this kid and all his friends.

And then, out of the blue, he asked again, "What's your name?"

Sticking with the fire-department conversation, she headed him off once more. "So what kind of calls do you get?"

He paused for a moment, thinking. Bug wondered whether he was going to make up something, but he seemed believable so far.

"Well, yesterday, for instance, there was some danger of a fire due to a suspected hot spot in a kitchen. The rest of the crews were busy and they called me in to keep an eye on it. So what's your name?"

Cool. This guy really does fight fires, thought Bug, once more ignoring the name request.

"Neat. Did it end up catching fire?"

"Almost. I got to it in time, though. The chief was pretty happy I was around."

In her mind, Bug imagined flames bursting out of a wall, setting curtains and shelves on fire while this kid named Frogger stood there spraying everything down with a . . . a hose? A fire extinguisher?

He reached for his pager again, but Bug playfully tugged it back.

"What's your name?" he asked for about the tenth time.

"BUG!" bellowed Walter.

Startled, Bug looked sharply around, but she couldn't see Walter at first.

"Bug! Bug! Over here," called Walter, jogging toward her. Befuddled, Bug released her grasp on the pager and turned to watch her father's approach.

Bug Revealed

For a few seconds, Bug almost forgot that Frogger was standing next to her as she watched Walter hustling across the track in his flapping shorts and calf-slapping cowboy boots. Looking at his bright tie-dyed shirt, sheepskin vest and brimless embroidered hat, she felt a slight blush warming her cheeks.

Embarrassing parent.

Embarrassing name.

Embarrassing shoe business.

"Bug?" echoed Frogger. "You were making fun of *my* name?"

But Bug was no longer listening to him. Walter had hurried past them without pausing, and she turned to follow in his wake. As far as she was concerned, the name conversation was over. There was work to be done, and the sooner they finished it, the sooner they could move on. She joined her father, who had plunked himself down on the ground beside

71

the broken television set, which he was now using as a table.

Walter had scrounged a large piece of white cardboard and a marker from the church ladies' bingo tent to make their sign. He threw out a number of suggestions that Bug rejected as too dumb. She had no patience for any lighthearted brainstorming right now.

"Just write, 'Shoes $5 Each. See Shoe-Girl Freak for Details,'" she grumbled.

Bug's mood was darkening, but Walter didn't seem to notice. When he had a scheme, no matter how far-fetched, he was unstoppably enthusiastic. Today was no different.

"Bug, this is going to be great."

It was then that he spotted Frogger, hovering in the background.

"Hey, I remember you." He jumped up and gave the boy a hearty handshake, thanking him profusely for convincing Doc Timmerman to admit them to the fairground.

Apparently, Doc had been about to send Walter packing when he asked Frogger what he thought about the crazy shoe scheme. Frogger had been so excited about the idea that Doc had decided to let them in. Walter was obviously of the opinion that Frogger had saved the day.

Frogger downplayed his role and gave Walter the credit. "It's the truth," Frogger said. "Single shoes make a lot of sense." Bug watched the two of them in disbelief, amazed that they could get so worked up about a pile of unwanted, unmatched, unnecessary shoes.

"Welcome to Tichville," Bug groaned. "Home of the One-Shoe Wonders."

"Tich*burg*," said Frogger quietly, not realizing that Bug was being sarcastic.

"Bug, ease up," laughed Walter. "This kid, what's your name, son? He's a valuable acquaintance. By the way, what's your name, son?"

"Don't tell him your name," she warned Frogger. "We'll be here for hours."

They both ignored her, and Frogger plunged ahead with the story of how he came by his unique name, happy to have found an interested audience. When he had finished, Walter said, "That is truly fascinating, Frogger."

"Oh, brother," Bug sighed.

"Did Bug tell you how she got her name?"

"Walter . . ." pleaded Bug, but there was no stopping him.

"It's really quite simple. She was a pest. Always buzzing around like an insect, but we couldn't call her mosquito or horsefly, and . . ."

Bug held her breath, hoping he wouldn't mention her real name. Belinda had to be the worst name on the face of the earth.

" . . . actually, she's more of a pest now," Walter laughed uproariously. "Back then, she was just as cute as a bug."

Frogger was smiling uncertainly, suddenly aware that this was clearly a sensitive issue with Bug.

"Don't you have a fire to put out or something?" Bug asked him peevishly, hoping to move him along.

Frogger stammered, "W-well, there's a pie-eating contest that starts right after the parade, and I promised to go in it."

Bug hooted. "You're kidding. A pie-eating contest? Will

73

there be a seed-spitting competition after that?" She was talking with a country twang she must have picked up from a television program.

"Maybe a greased-hog rassling match?" She flashed Walter a look of utter desperation. "Oh, man, get me out of here."

As Frogger picked up his bicycle to leave, Walter hurried over to fetch the box with the RetroTred Hoopsters they had set aside earlier. The boy was clearly excited when he saw them, and even Bug had to admit that the green and red shoes were not bad.

Frogger pulled them on, grinning from ear to ear. Then he performed an intricate series of basketball maneuvers, jumping and pivoting, pretending to dribble a ball, as Walter cheered loudly and clapped his approval and a few passersby stopped to watch. The two pig-guys halted in the middle of assembling the final length of feeding trough to look on and chuckle.

But neither Walter nor Frogger seemed to mind. They were both so pleased with each other's company and with the fabulous shoes that something as trivial as making a public spectacle didn't even register. In fact, the only awkward moment arose when Frogger began to climb on his bicycle to ride away.

"Aren't you forgetting something, son?" asked Walter gently.

Frogger looked bewildered until Bug explained that her father expected to be paid for the shoes.

If he was disappointed that the RetroTreds were not a gift, he didn't show it and quickly handed over the money to Walter.

"It's been a pleasure doing business with you, Frogger," boomed Walter as the boy rode away. Turning to Bug, he waved two five-dollar bills and sang, "We're in the money, honey. We're in the money . . ."

Two down and 998 to go, thought Bug. It was going to be a long day.

Shoe Sign

After Frogger left, Walter and Bug turned their attention to their sign. Bug rejected "Sports Shoe Boo-Boos," "The Shoe Zoo" and "The Shoe Stew" and convinced Walter to keep it simple. They finally agreed on "The Shoe Pile."

"You're right, of course. Simple but effective," Walter declared, handing Bug the marker. "You do it. Your printing is neater than mine."

"Walter, those cows over there could print neater than you," she teased. "Shouldn't we put the price on too?"

"Absolutely. Otherwise, we'll talk ourselves hoarse explaining the deal. What about, '$5 each or $10 a pair'?"

"We're still going to talk ourselves hoarse trying to explain this to everyone, but it's a start," Bug said, carefully printing each letter.

Walter went next door to the pig-guys and borrowed a hammer and two nails, then lifted Bug onto his shoulders so that she could hang the sign as high as possible. But Walter had trouble getting a good foothold on the constantly shifting pile of shoes, so Bug gripped the pole with her legs and arms and carefully shinnied up like a monkey. Walter hovered beneath her to catch her if she lost her grip, but the only thing that fell was the hammer, which barely missed his head. After he retrieved the hammer and handed it back to Bug, he decided just to stand back and offer advice.

"That's good. A bit higher. More to the left," he instructed. Bug was holding on for dear life with her legs and just wanted to get the sign nailed in anywhere, any way she could. Once the second nail was sunk, she slowly slid down, relieved to be finished.

"It's a bit crooked," observed Walter. Catching a sour look from Bug, he hastily added, "But it looks great. Sort of catches the eye when it's slightly askew. Good job. Honest."

Laughing, Bug picked up a neon-purple cross-trainer and threw it at him. He caught it and tossed it back, then scooped up several more, pitching them underhand in a barrage that sent Bug scurrying to the far side of the shoe pile, where she ducked and hopped from one foot to the other, dodging the airborne runners.

The shoe fight came to an abrupt end with the arrival of an entire women's baseball team.

"Hey, handsome, you've got a pretty good pitching arm for a cowboy in shorts."

Walter turned to face a short, stocky woman in a baseball uniform, a bat in one hand and a catcher's mitt on the other. Her name tag said "Ruby." A dozen or more team members

77

stood behind her, grinning. Taking in Walter's wildly colored shirt and sheepskin vest, Ruby added, "Or a hippie."

"Neither, I'm afraid. Just a guy with a ton of one-of-a-kind shoes to sell. Need any?"

"Honey, if it'll help our game, we'll buy the whole pile. What's the deal?"

"Five bucks apiece. Just wade on in, and see what you can find." He quickly explained that they were all brand-new but didn't match. Ruby made a loud pop with the gum she was chewing and pointed to a shoe Walter was holding, one he had been about to launch at Bug.

"That green and orange one there. Is it a ball shoe?"

"Well, Ruby, the Doubleheader here might be just what you need. It's light and has good support, and the soft cleats give you lots of grip but won't hurt anyone when you slide." He paused and looked at her admiringly. "A gal like you could run bases all day in a pair of these."

Bug had watched Walter in his sales-pitch mode before and knew he was good, but with an audience of women, he really sizzled. One part information, nine parts flirtation. Selling merchandise to those of the female persuasion, he often said, was like asking for a date.

"We're not allowed to slide," said Ruby. "This is a just-for-fun league. Trouble is, we're too busy having fun and never seem to win." The rest of the team laughed and nodded in agreement, closing in around Ruby to examine the shoe.

"Looks more like a golf shoe," cracked one of the women.

Walter smiled broadly and handed the Doubleheader to Ruby, who dropped her bat and glove to take it. "You're right," he said. "Sports shoes are really looking more fashionable these days. A bit wild for some, but I know a few semipro ballplayers who swear by these."

Downright ugly was how Bug would describe the shoe, but a quick calculation of a dozen women buying 24 shoes at $5 each inspired her to join in.

"You want to try on a pair?" she asked, looking down at Ruby's feet. "About a five?"

"Good guess, darling. That'd be a start, unless this gentleman has one of those slider things that measures your feet."

"Ruby," Walter laughed heartily, "we don't even have a chair." Halfway up the pile, Bug found a red, left-footed Doubleheader, size five, and tossed it to Walter, who loosened the laces and tongue before handing it to Ruby with a dramatic flourish.

As she took the shoe from Walter, Ruby curtsied and said, "Now I know what Cinderella must have felt like. You're charming — I'll give you that. You're not a prince, too, are you?"

Bug rolled her eyes, but Walter took it in stride, as if Ruby were the cleverest woman he had ever met. "I'm afraid not, my dear. And I don't think we have a single glass slipper left in the pile."

"Are you sure?" one of the women asked, giggling like a schoolgirl.

Walter turned to Bug, hoping she would get involved in this playful banter, but she inflated her cheeks, pressed her fingers to her lips and held her stomach, pretending she was about to barf.

"My assistant says, 'No,'" he chortled. "But you ladies are welcome to have a look yourself. Climb on in."

The Mop Shop Belles, sponsored by Ruby's own hair and nail salon, spent the next 15 minutes rummaging around knee-deep in the pile of shoes in search of bargain footwear. Before they left, their opponents from Wamble, the Drain Surgeons, sponsored by Jack's Main Drain Service, had joined in the hunt as well. By the time the two teams threw their first pitch on the ball diamond, Bug and Walter were up $270.

"Can you believe this?" Walter exclaimed. "They loved it. Didn't I tell you this was a great idea? Didn't I?"

"Yeah, you did. But look at the mess they made. Some of them even left their old shoes behind."

One Shoe at a Time

That visit by Ruby and her teammates set the tone for the rest of the morning. Every hour, another ball game started, bringing with it new players and dozens of spectators, all of whom were eager to do a little shoe diving to find the deal of a lifetime. Walter was ecstatic, urging Bug in and around the pile time after time to dig out that all-important first shoe which would lure a new customer into the exciting hunt for a second.

Within a couple of hours, they had sold more than 200 shoes, and Walter's pockets were bulging with wads of 5- and 10-dollar bills. Word of The Shoe Pile quickly spread from the baseball diamond to the rest of the fairground, and Bug was constantly surrounded by a dozen or more customers. There was no time to take a break, and much to Bug's dismay, many of the bargain hunters insisted on telling her the story of their various foot ailments.

One such customer was a stout woman with gargantuan

feet and fat toes. Sitting in a wheelchair like a queen on her throne, she cackled gleefully as she ordered her tiny husband back and forth for over half an hour. The slight, rather fragile-looking man patiently did as he was told, struggling to fit a variety of oversized basketball and tennis shoes on her feet. She bought five shoes in total, calling Bug "dearie" as she pressed $25 into her hand.

"He ruined my feet, he did, dearie," she exclaimed. "When I married him, I was quite the dancer, but he stepped on my toes every Saturday night for the first 20 years of our marriage, and look at them now." She paused, staring off into the distance, no doubt recalling her glorious ballroom days, then added, "But he's paying the price for his clumsiness now, isn't he? Has to wheel me everywhere we go. And you can be sure we don't go far anymore."

Bug could understand why as she watched the little red-faced man huff and puff his way across the rutted grass in the direction of the grandstand. His wife, easily twice his size, took full advantage of their slow progress, calling out to her friends and applying the wheelchair's brakes without warning whenever she wanted to stop for a chat.

Bug had never seen so many different characters in one place. There were few kids her age but lots of adults, many of them old and weather-beaten. Some were dressed in their work clothes, while others were treating fair day as a special outing. Most of the men — and some of the women — wore baseball caps that advertised plumbing services and seed companies or farm suppliers. There was no shortage of roly-poly women attired in sweatpants or polyester shorts,

82

accompanied by equally rotund men in baggy blue jeans or green work pants.

There were lots of younger families too, with babies in strollers and toddlers in wagons. As the mothers waded into the sprawling mound of shoes, hyperactive kids, revved up on cotton candy and taffy apples, ran around the edge of the pile, playing tag and wrestling one another to the ground. The men hung back talking in small groups until it was time to venture forward with their wallets to settle up for their families' collection of unmatched footwear.

As the sun rose higher in the sky, Bug's stomach started to growl. The bowl of oatmeal at Betty's Burger 'N Bait this morning seemed like ancient history, and she wished they had brought some sandwiches and drinks for lunch. Bug generally wasn't a big eater, but it had been a long, tiring morning. It wasn't even noon yet, but she had been working hard.

Knowing that Walter was always ready to eat, she called over to him as he was closing a sale for six hiking shoes. "Hey, I'm starving. Any chance of a lunch break?"

Walter made his way around a heavyset man balancing on one foot as he wrestled the other into a bright green golf shoe. "Sounds like a good idea," he replied, wiping the sweat off his forehead, "but we'll have to take it in shifts. Things don't look as if they're going to slow down anytime soon." He had removed his vest and replaced the cowboy boots with a pair of slipperlike rock-climbing shoes. One was red, the other orange, and he looked like an oversized elf in them. His beard completed the cartoon image. He reached into his pocket, pulled out a crumpled 20-dollar bill and handed it to Bug.

"Get what you want, then have a look around and stretch your legs a bit while you have the chance. But don't be too long. And would you please bring back something interesting to eat?"

That should be easy enough here in ICHBURG, Bug thought. She noted that Walter hadn't said "good" or "healthy" — just "interesting."

Woolly Encounters

Before Bug could ease her way through the crowd of shoe customers, she was stopped by a freckle-faced woman anxious to find junior-sized basketball high-tops for her three boys. Bug pointed her in Walter's direction, then quickly headed away from The Shoe Pile.

A baseball game had just ended, and dozens of spectators were making their way to and from the ball diamond, creating a confusion of human currents. But a life in the city had taught Bug how to spot openings in a crowd and slip fluidly into them without even slowing her pace. She paused briefly at the edge of the racetrack, checking for traffic and horses, then hurried across.

Skirting a knot of people who had stopped to admire a happy couple's new baby, Bug found herself walking away from the midway toward the livestock display. She hurried past pens of cows, goats and sheep, all being primped by their young owners in preparation for the 4-H animal-judging contest.

Bug's mind was on food, though, and she barely glanced in their direction. She was looking for the shortest route to take her back toward the midway and the food concessions. As she paused at the end of the stable's center aisle, two little boys tore past her, almost knocking her off her feet.

"Wait for me, stupid head," yelled the slower of the two, although they were both moving fast. Bug did a double take as she realized they were identical twins, right down to the clothes they wore. She watched as first one, then the other clambered up the rails of one of the pens and dropped into an enclosure filled with sheep.

Seconds later, a woman in a stylish denim pantsuit raced by in pursuit of the boys. The high heels and long, pointy toes of her designer boots hindered her progress over the rough ground, and she struggled to keep her balance.

"Boys, stop there. Right now," she called loudly. "Kenny! Kerry! You're making mommy very angry."

Without pausing for breath, one of the twins jumped onto the back of a startled sheep, grabbing fistfuls of the animal's wool to steady himself. The second twin tried to climb aboard behind him, whining, "Kennnnny. Let me ride toooooo!"

But the sheep had had enough of the rambunctious twins. It lunged forward and whirled, throwing the rider clear and sending the other twin into a corner of the enclosure. Both boys started howling in unison as their mother reached the pen.

"Oh, my poor babies. Mommy told you to stay away from

these filthy, dangerous animals. Now come out of there right this minute."

A concerned-looking man had hurried up to the sheep pen just in time to see the boys become airborne. He quickly unlatched the gate and stepped in to retrieve the twins.

"Oh, there you are, Dunston," scolded the woman. "Really, dear, you have to move a bit faster, or the boys are going to do themselves serious harm. Just look at them."

A half-dozen terrified, bleating sheep were dashing about the pen in a panic while the wailing boys scrambled through the straw to reach the safety of their father's outstretched arms. He scooped them both up and carried them out of the pen, leaving the gate wide-open behind him. As the twins' mother started to pick straw from the boys' hair, the sheep bolted toward the open gate.

Were it not for Bug's lightning-quick reaction, the sheep would have escaped. She lunged for the gate, pushing and holding it shut before the lead sheep could squeeze through the gap. The boys' father lowered the twins to the ground and helped fasten the gate.

"Say, you're pretty fast, young lady," he remarked. "Do you babysit by any chance?"

Before Bug could explain that she didn't live around here — or that the boys probably needed a zookeeper instead — Kenny and Kerry were on the move again.

"I want cotton candy," shouted the one in the lead.

"I want cotton candy too," yelled the other as they raced toward the midway with their parents in tow.

As he hustled off, the father called back, "We're the

Troths. Over on Riverview Road. The big brick house by the river. Give us a call. Always looking for a babysitter."

I just bet you are, thought Bug. Oh, yeah.

Mistaken Identity

As she headed toward the food concessions, Bug spotted Frogger making his way down from the grandstand. The pie-eating contest must have just ended. His face was smeared with yellow pie filling, and his hair stood in stiff peaks, held in place with dried meringue. She wondered how he'd done but resisted the urge to call out to him. After all, she didn't have much time and was not about to waste any of it talking to a gooey-faced junior firefighter with a pink pager.

The small midway was packed with fairgoers. Every adult seemed to have a clutch of children, and it appeared that every child was wielding something sticky — taffy apples, brightly colored Frostee-Freezes in paper cones or pink and blue cotton candy. At the far end of the grass avenue, excited kids waited in front of the rides, hopping and twirling about, barely able to contain themselves, while the nearer end held a strip of food vendors.

Lines of people snaked about in all directions, and anyone passing down the midway was forced to squeeze in and out of clusters of friends, neighbors and families. Below the shrill music blaring from the rides and the popcorn stands was the low murmur of dozens of conversations, constantly interrupted by shrieks of recognition and boisterous greetings.

As she skirted the bumper of a french-fry truck, Bug was approached by three tiny elderly ladies all wearing bright print dresses and wide-brimmed straw hats. One of them pointed a white-gloved finger directly in her face and squealed, "Why, if it isn't Claire Hinch's granddaughter. Just look at her, will you? Growing like a weed."

Startled to have been singled out, Bug stopped in her tracks. The ladies bustled in for a closer look, almost pinning her against a big propane tank at the side of the chip truck. Before she could say a word, a second member of the trio said, "You're right, of course, Agnes. Would you look at those eyes? Just like her mother's."

"Not the eyes, my dear. That nose is the clincher. That saucy little Hinch nose. You can spot it a mile away."

The third old lady, quiet until now, gave a delicate sniff and contemplated Bug carefully.

"Betsy, isn't it?" she asked.

"Uh, no, ma'am," Bug replied. "My name's . . ."

"Oh, you don't have to tell us," the first interrupted. "We never forget a name."

"Hardly ever," added the second.

"Holly," proclaimed the third triumphantly. "Definitely Holly."

"Oh, no, no, no, no, no," spluttered Agnes. "You're thinking of Cornellia Newcombe's daughter. Snooty little thing. She must be married by now. Not as pretty as this one, either."

Bug looked from one face to another. By this time, the women were so engrossed in their discussion about her possible parentage that they were paying no mind to her, and she wondered whether she could slip away. But pressed up against the truck with the three little ladies clustered around her, she had no chance of escape.

Agnes had just decided that Bug might not be a Hinch after all — maybe a Thompson, one of Earl Thompson's children's children, the one that lived out on Hog's Back Road — when a scruffy old man flourishing a cane barged into their midst.

"Ladies, ladies, ladies. Even though I haven't lived in these parts for 15 years, I can still tell a Hinch from a Newcombe or a Thompson, believe you me. 'N trust me, this here lil girlie doesn't belong ta any of 'em. I don't know her name, but I can assure ya she hasn't been in Tichburg for more than three or four hours. She's the girl from that pile of shoes down near the ball diamond, 'n yer keeping her from her lunch. Now, if you ladies will excuse us, we're gonna get ourselves a bite ta eat."

Taking Bug's hand in one beefy paw, he led her away from the truck. As they walked out onto the midway, he called back over his shoulder, "And there's some excellent shoes ta be bought down there, so I suggest ya skip right over 'n take a gander."

Bug smiled at the ladies and shrugged helplessly, walking

alongside the old man without a word. Her eyes cast to the ground, she noticed he was wearing one mauve and one black jogging shoe, and she knew she had just been rescued by a satisfied customer.

Blueberry Pie

They passed several burger stands and candy stalls, then cut across the midway to a large tent filled with dozens of picnic tables and a crush of people.

A large banner overhead indicated that they were entering the pie tent of the Women's Christian Temperance Union (Tichburg Chapter, Est. 1887). If the long lineup was any indication, the pies must be first-rate.

As the old gent surveyed the scene, Bug said, "Thanks a lot, sir, for helping me out back there, but I'd better get going. My dad is expecting me back soon."

He touched the brim of his beat-up straw fedora and tipped his head slightly toward Bug. "Cigar Davis at yer service, young lady. I bought a pair of shoes from yer daddy an hour ago, 'n I've been in hog heaven ever since. Yessiree-bob. Like walkin' on air. Figure I owe ya a piece o' pie."

"No, really, that's OK," Bug protested. But before she

93

could say another word, Cigar had handed her his cane and was pushing his way into the crowd around the serving table.

* * *

He was back in less than five minutes, clutching two large cups of lemonade against his chest and carrying two paper plates weighed down with humongous slabs of blueberry pie topped with ice cream.

"Yer an excellent guest, my dear," he cackled as he set the pie and lemonade on a nearby table. "I woulda had ta stand there fer a half hour, but when I tol' everyone you wuz The Shoe Pile Girl, why, they just let me go ta the head o' the line."

"Really?" Bug asked, unsure whether the benefits of being known as "The Shoe Pile Girl" could ever outweigh the embarrassment factor.

"Yessiree. Everybody knows how busy ya must be. Yer a bit of a celebrity — 'n they wantcha ta be able ta get back ta business."

This is way too weird, thought Bug, glancing over at the crowded serving area. Sure enough, a half-dozen people were looking her way. One elderly gentleman lifted his foot in the air and shook a bright green RetroTred at her. She smiled shyly and gave him a slight finger waggle.

"C'mon, let's get out o' here," said Cigar. He took his cane from Bug and gestured for her to bring the lemonade and pie. Bug balanced a pie plate on top of each cup, then held her breath as she gingerly picked up the cups, fearing a catastrophic spill in front of her new fans. Moving carefully, she followed Cigar to a side exit.

Once outside in the sunlight, Cigar paused and briefly

looked around. "There she is," he announced, pointing to a huge pink granite boulder not far from where they stood. He made a beeline for it.

When Bug caught up to him, Cigar was leaning against — almost sitting on — the gigantic rock, his cane lying on the ground beside him. He relieved Bug of her load and motioned for her to climb up. Once she was sitting cross-legged, he handed her a drink and a plate. Then he dug two plastic forks from his shirt pocket and passed one to her.

Sitting partway up a gently sloping hill, the boulder afforded a great view of the bustling midway. Behind them was a field of parked cars. The grandstand towered above them on one side, and a series of low concrete-block buildings stood to their left. A steady stream of visitors passed in and out of the nearest one, whose sign declared it the Kitchen 'N Craft Shed.

Bug set her drink down and took a bite of the most heavenly pie she had ever tasted — moist, ripe berries nestled in a sweet, flaky crust. She took two more big bites and then sipped her lemonade. It was actually peaceful here, even though the crowd was not far away.

"Where ya from?" Cigar asked. "Ya look like a city kid. I suppose ya shouldn't be talkin' ta strangers."

"Well," sighed Bug, "if I didn't talk to strangers here, I guess I wouldn't be talking to anyone. In fact, everybody in this place seems a bit strange."

Cigar laughed good-naturedly. To Bug, he looked like your standard-issue old country coot: plaid farmer's shirt with rolled-up sleeves, baggy pants held up by red suspenders and a well-worn straw hat. Only his unmatched jogging shoes were new. As he pushed his hat back off his forehead, she noticed he had a raggedy brush cut that extended from his head to his beard.

"Seems that everybody knows everybody else around here," said Bug. "Except me, of course."

"Oh, they all know ya by now," chuckled Cigar. "I grew up here. Left about 15 years ago, 'n just got back yesterday. But I betcha I know most of the people down there, or at least their folks. Funny how things don't seem ta change much around here — not like in the city."

"You're right about the city, I guess," said Bug. "Yesterday morning, I was having breakfast in my own apartment, and 12 hours later, I was sleeping in a truck on my way to nowhere."

"This ain't exactly nowhere."

"Well, it's not anywhere I ever planned on being."

"Plans change sometimes." Cigar scooped some pie and ice cream into his mouth before continuing. "So where ya stayin'?"

"Nowhere," answered Bug. "I guess we're homeless. It's hard to tell with Walter."

"Walter? That yer daddy's name?"

"Yeah. We just packed everything up and took off. He's got some idea about moving to the country, and here we are."

"An idea man, is he? Likes to follow his dreams?"

"More like nightmares," laughed Bug. She dug into her pie and finished it off in four bites.

"Ahhh, livin' in a small town's not so bad. Take Tichburg, fer instance. Not many secrets in a place this size. People are

96

friendly, at least most of 'em. Ya jes avoid the troublesome ones 'n enjoy the rest.

"Mind ya, it can be tough bein' the new kid," he continued. "At first, anyway. I wuz new here 'bout 80 years back. Took a few lickin's from the other kids fer a while, but if ya stay in a place long enough, people come ta accept ya."

"You got beat up because you were new?" asked Bug.

"Oh, that wuz jes the way it wuz in them days," explained Cigar. "People didn't take much to changes back then. It's different now."

"How old were you?"

"Only about 6, I reckon."

"So what'd you do when they tried to beat you up?"

"I used ta fight back some 'n hide some. Used ta come up here 'n sit on this rock a lot jes to be alone. My daddy — well, my adopted daddy — found me sittin' here cryin' one day after some kids had chased me through town. Told me ta quit feelin' sorry fer myself. Said, 'That rock yer sittin' on has been here 'bout 10,000 years, through blizzard 'n flood. Compared to that, everyone here is a newcomer.' And he wuz right. After a bit, people find someone else to pick on. They may never forget ya weren't born here, but they accept ya all the same."

"Well, I don't plan to be here long enough for that," announced Bug, jumping down from the rock. She finished her lemonade and gathered up her plate and fork. "We're outta here tonight."

Cigar nodded his head thoughtfully, then said, "Ya goin' back ta sell some more shoes now?"

97

"Yep. The more we sell, the sooner we'll get wherever we're going."

Bug began to walk away but paused, then turned to face Cigar, still leaning comfortably against his rock. "Thanks for the pie."

"Don't mention it," he said. "I'll see ya around."

Acceptance

Bug was making her way back to The Shoe Pile when she got caught up in a surge of excited people rushing toward the track. Apparently, there had been an accident during a race. Someone had been trampled by a horse. A mother with two young children. All around her, people talked gravely, swapping snippets of information as they headed for the scene of the accident.

As Bug moved down the hill with the crowd, she suddenly realized she'd forgotten to get Walter some lunch, but there was no turning back now. She was a passenger in a moving body of people.

At the track, she worked her way to the front of the crowd, where a line of men wearing Tichburg Volunteer Fire Department T-shirts held people back from an ancient-looking ambulance. The vehicle must have been as old as Walter's dump truck, although it was in much better condition.

Its rear doors were open, and a woman was being strapped onto a stretcher while a man hovered over her nervously.

Bug inched her way closer for a better look, then gasped in surprise. She knew the man and woman. It was the couple with the hyperactive twins from the sheep pen. She glanced around quickly, looking for the two boys. They were standing on either side of Frogger, whose pie-smeared face was now coated in a layer of dust.

As word filtered through the crowd that there had been no serious injuries, there was a collective sigh of relief and people started to drift away.

"Fool woman stepped right in front of the horse," a man explained to his wife. "It's a wonder she wasn't killed."

"She probably would have been if it weren't for that young Archibald boy," said another, pointing to Frogger. "He saved her life. Pulled her back in the nick of time. More or less just tackled her and threw her to the ground. Darnedest thing I ever saw."

So Frogger's a hero, Bug thought, looking over at him. People were congratulating him, slapping him on the back as they passed by. Somewhat the worse for wear, with his grimy face and red and green RetroTred Hoopsters, Frogger certainly didn't look like your typical comic-book hero.

This is one crazy place, all right, Bug concluded, walking across the track as the ambulance pulled away with its lights flashing and siren wailing.

* * *

Walter had little information to add to what Bug already knew about the incident other than business had ground to a halt when people had rushed over to have a closer look. During the lull, he had managed to haul their mattresses out from under the shrinking pile of shoes and drag them back up into the truck. He had also retrieved some wayward footwear. After a morning of shopping frenzy, shoes had been flung every which way. Walter had even had to crawl under the dump truck to get a few and pick some out of the neighboring pig-trough display.

There was little time for small talk. Bug had just apologized for not bringing Walter something to eat when they found themselves surrounded by eager bargain hunters, several of whom were asking for green and red RetroTreds just like the ones Frogger Archibald was wearing during his dramatic rescue of the lady on the track.

Bug had been back at work for about 30 minutes when a man wearing a fire department ball cap and T-shirt roared up on a four-wheel all-terrain vehicle, scattering a cluster of 8-year-old ballplayers in all directions. Leaving the red Honda idling, he beckoned Walter over and shouted above the noise: "Doc says you need an official sign for your shoe sale, 'cause you're doing such a good business."

He reached behind to the ATV's carrier rack and pulled out a neatly printed, plastic-coated sign that announced "THE SHOE PILE" in huge red block letters. He handed it to Walter. "Doc says I gotta hang this one and to be sure it's straight."

While Walter gazed at the sign admiringly, the volunteer firefighter threw his machine into reverse, dispersing a family of shoppers bent over the shoe pile, and backed up to the base of the utility pole, wheeling over a dozen shoes on the way. He wrestled to unhook several bungee cords, freeing a small ladder from the carrier rack. Balancing the foot of the ladder on the back of the ATV, he leaned the top precariously against the pole.

The man removed a hammer and some nails from a small toolbox. Walter passed him the sign. A minute later, the crooked piece of cardboard had been replaced with the computer-printed board, fresh and neat and square. The sign man quickly strapped the ladder to the ATV and stepped back to survey his handiwork.

"Doc says he'll swing by later to say hello — and collect the $50 you owe." And with that, he climbed back onto the ATV and took off in a cloud of dust.

"Now that does look terrific," Walter beamed. "But how did he know it was called The Shoe Pile? And that our old sign was crooked?"

Looking around, Bug finally spotted a gleaming white pickup truck sitting at the top of a low rise on the far side of the racetrack. Although the man standing in the bed of the truck was little more than a speck from this distance, she could feel his eyes on them — staring through his binoculars.

She pointed him out to Walter, who grinned and saluted the ever watchful Doc Timmerman.

"You know, Bug, I think we're going to like it here," said Walter, turning back to their customers. "People are really considerate."

The Jerk

The next hour passed quickly until Walter announced that he could go no longer without food. He pulled a crumpled wad of five-dollar bills out of his pocket and gave them to Bug so that she could make change in his absence, then hurried across the track and up the hill toward the food stands. Bug had told him about the pie tent, and he said he'd bring her back another piece.

Trouble arrived within minutes of his departure, in the form of a teenage boy leaning against the back of Walter's truck.

At first, Bug paid little attention to the boy. She was busy with customers, trying hard to concentrate on handling the money from some while explaining to others, for what seemed like the millionth time, that the shoes were never, ever going to match.

But when he climbed up onto the side of the truck, Bug stared at the chunky teenager. He looked familiar, which seemed strange, because she didn't know anyone — other than Cigar, Frogger, the crazy twins' family . . . and Betty from the diner. That was it, of course. He was the creepy-looking guy who worked at the gas station next to Betty's Burger 'N Bait, the one who had triggered her jerk alarm back in Wamble.

"Hey, get down from there," she shouted.

He ignored her.

"I said, get down," she called again, upset enough not to worry about the consequences of yelling at someone much bigger and older than she was.

Still ignoring her, he lifted a corner of the blue tarpaulin to peer inside.

A burst of adrenaline rushed through Bug's body, making her tremble with nervous energy. "Get off that truck!" she yelled, punctuating her demand by throwing a hiking shoe full force at his backside. The shoe curved wide to the left and bounced off the truck but was quickly followed by a volley of three more. The final one, a pink and white bowling shoe, connected, glancing off his right leg. He jumped down and whirled around to face Bug.

Despite the heat of the day, he was dressed all in black — T-shirt, low-slung jeans and cowboy boots — which merely emphasized his greasy hair and pale, pimply complexion. Bug figured he was probably about five years older than she was, with a soft, lumpy body that indicated too much junk food and not enough exercise.

"Why'd ya go do that, shrimp?" he demanded. "I was just looking to see if you had anything else for sale. Like a truckload of socks with holes in them to go with your stupid shoes." He smirked, looking pleased with himself, convinced that he had just uttered something incredibly witty.

As he spoke, he dug the heel of his boot into the pink and white bowling shoe and ground it into the grass until it was covered with bright green stains. Then he picked it up and tossed it back onto the pile.

"That one's wrecked," he said. "Better sell it half price."

He turned and began to walk away. Bug sighed in relief. Then he spotted a friend over by the baseball diamond's bleachers and stopped.

"Hey, Cecil!" he yelled.

Cecil, a dull-looking teen, gazed around vacantly, trying to locate the person who was calling him. The gas jockey jumped back up onto the side of the dump truck and called again, waving a shoe that had landed on top of the tarpaulin.

"Come on over here, and I'll buy you a shoe."

His friend shrugged in confusion.

"A shoe, you moron. C'mon over."

Bug could feel tears welling up in her eyes and tried to blink them back, determined not to let this jerk see that he was getting to her. She turned to take some money from a little girl who had been standing quietly beside her, waiting to pay.

"That's Nicky Knowlton," she said, as she handed her money to Bug. "He's mean to everybody."

Bug nodded and tried to ignore the bully, who was now calling out like a carnival barker.

"Ladies and gentlemen, step right up and see the amazing pile of shoes. Big ones. Small ones. And everything in between. But watch out for the shoe troll that guards them. Get too close, and she'll hit you with one of them."

He was fully into his lame patter now, hanging off the side of the truck. His friend Cecil arrived, accompanied by a scrawnier version of himself — both looked to be about 16 or 17 years old. They began laughing and poking each other, urging Nicky on.

Bug had seen their kind before. They filled the park benches along Clancy Street back home, roughhousing and yelling at passersby out of sheer boredom and meanness, ready to cause trouble at the slightest provocation.

Uncertain of what to do, Bug had moved off to the side, into the shadow of the pig-trough display, and anyone approaching The Shoe Pile might have thought that Nicky was, indeed, in charge. But Nicky was not attracting many people, except for a handful of little boys who had temporarily lost interest in the ball game. Everyone else was averting his or her eyes and quickly moving on, embarrassed by the local bully but unwilling to stand up to him. He might not be smart, but Nicky was spiteful, and most residents of Tichburg knew he was capable of all sorts of malicious mischief.

"C'mon down, Nicky," called Cecil. "We're going to ride the Tilt-O'-Whirl."

"Are you kidding?" scoffed Nicky. "Why pay when you can do the shoe dive for free?" With that, he released his grip on the truck, jumped down and took a running leap into the pile of shoes, sending them flying in all directions. Pretending he was in water, he rolled and flopped to the edge of the pile, where his friends stood.

Scooping up a small white tennis shoe as he rose, Nicky tossed it to the top of the pile and called out to the young boys who had been watching him intently, "First one to get that shoe wins a prize."

The kids hesitated for a split second, looking from Nicky to the top of the pile, then dove in, grabbing one another and rolling and scrambling around like preschoolers in a tank of plastic balls. To liven up the action, Nicky and his sidekicks began throwing shoes at them, instigating a full-fledged shoe fight. The situation was rapidly spinning out of control, and Bug was at a loss to stop them.

Just then, Doc Timmerman steered his white pickup off the racetrack and rolled slowly across the grass toward Nicky and his friends. They were unaware of his arrival until he honked the horn sharply.

As Nicky turned and saw Doc, the jeering look quickly disappeared from his face. Doc stared at him unblinkingly with a look that could have melted steel.

"You boys need a ride out of here?"

"No, sir," Nicky replied. "Just having some fun. But we're going now. There's nothing here in our size."

The trio walked away without looking back, crossed the track and turned toward the midway.

Doc nodded curtly at Bug and asked, "Where's your daddy?"

Bug motioned toward the midway, unsure of what to say about what had just happened.

"Well, I came by to pick up the $50 exhibitor's fee, but I can come back a little bit later to see him."

"It's all right," she replied quickly. "I've got it here." She dug into her pocket and pulled out a handful of folded bills. She counted out 10 fives, walked over to Doc's pickup and passed the money to him through the driver's window.

In one simple motion, Doc folded the bills between his fingers and slipped them into his shirt pocket. "Much obliged," he said, touching the brim of his cowboy hat, then slipped the truck quietly into gear and drove away.

Old-Fashioned Advice

A minute later, Cigar Davis came hustling over, moving as fast as his cane and the rough terrain would allow. He was wheezing slightly from the exertion and wiped the sweat from his brow with the back of his hand as he stood before Bug.

"I wuz over ta the far side o' the ballpark 'n I noticed those young hooligans givin' ya grief," he explained between huffs. "There wuz no call for 'em ta be teasin' ya like that."

Bug shrugged, relieved that the boys were gone and happy to see a friendly face. Her legs were still a bit trembly, but she no longer felt as if she were going to burst into tears.

"No matter where ya go, there'll always be punks like that who only want ta cause people misery. Once they cross yer path, ya need ta decide whether ya want ta avoid 'em or send 'em a message."

"A message?" Bug asked. "What kind of message?"

"A steer-clear-of-me-or-there'll-be-a-heapa-trouble message."
He poked at some stray shoes with his cane as he talked, pushing them closer to the pile. "Ya have ta figure out their weak spot 'n then come up with a way ta tickle it a bit. Just so's they know someone's keepin' an eye on 'em."

Cigar paused as he caught sight of Walter, who was walking toward them carrying an entire pie.

"But ya gotta go about it careful like, so's ya don't make matters worse."

Walter was grinning as he approached them. "You were right about the pie, Bug. It was so good, I bought a whole one — fresh peach. Eat what you like, and we'll have the rest later."

Nodding toward Cigar's mismatched joggers, he said, "So how are the feet, soldier?"

Cigar guffawed loudly. "Ya don't forget a thing, do ya?" Turning to Bug, he explained. "I tol' yer daddy I haven't owned a pair of really comfortable shoes since my army days — a long time ago.

"They fit a treat, young fella," he said to Walter. "If I had the funds, I'd buy another pair."

Fearing a request for a freebie, Walter quickly switched topics.

"Hey, did you see that Loose Goose Bingo?" he asked Bug. "Craziest game I've ever seen. There's this huge pen that's divided up into squares, like a bingo card, with a different number on each square. Then they turn this big old goose loose in the pen. Whenever it poops, the announcer calls the number of the square it hits."

110

Bug looked at Walter blankly. "And the point of this game is . . . ?" she asked.

Cigar answered. "Ya see, players choose four numbers, and whenever that goose, uh, picks one of their numbers, they get ta check it off. First one ta get all four numbers wins."

"That is so disgusting," harrumphed Bug.

"Kind of makes you glad you're in the shoe game, I suppose," Walter teased.

"Yeah, right."

* * *

When Walter noticed the shoes that had been flung away from the pile, Bug told him about Nicky Knowlton's visit and how Doc Timmerman had chased him off.

Walter shook his head and wrapped his arm around Bug's shoulders. "You know, when I was on my way to get something to eat, I saw that kid pull up and park that darn loud car of his behind the grandstand — in a handicapped parking spot, no less! He must have headed down here first to check out our shoes. Not much you can do about a creep like that, though."

"Well, I wish there were," replied Bug. "Guys like that deserve to get . . ." She paused, trying to think of a suitable punishment.

". . . deserve to get ignored," said Walter. "Bullies are best left alone, Bug. Remember that."

Cigar cleared his throat as if to say something, then changed his mind. He shifted his cane from one hand to the other, momentarily lost in thought.

"Well," he finally announced, "I best get back ta the fair. Gotta see a man about a goose. Young lady, if it's OK with yer daddy, why don't you meet me up by my old rock 'bout half an hour from now. See if ya can borrow a bit of grain from those guys next door to ya there, and we'll feed some o' the animals."

With that, he turned and made his way toward the track.

Payback Time

At a few minutes before 3:00, Bug closed a deal on three mixed pairs of fluorescent-colored aerobic shoes and told Walter that she was going to meet Cigar Davis for her break. Walter, busy with a customer, nodded and then reminded her to ask for some grain from the pig-guys next door.

The pig-guys were more than happy to give Bug a small bag of feed.

Feeling a bit hungry, Bug decided to take a piece of Walter's peach pie with her. He had left it sitting on the running board of the truck with a small plastic knife, but before she could cut off a hunk, she had to shoo away a half-dozen hornets hovering over it. A couple of the hornets buzzed angrily around her as she trotted across the track and up the hill to meet Cigar.

He was leaning against the big boulder, cradling a large, placid goose in his arms.

113

"Where'd you get that?" she asked.

"This here's Gerta. She's the star over at the Loose Goose Bingo," explained Cigar. "My old pal Freddie Holler has been runnin' that game fer 40 years now. When I tol' Freddie I wanted ta show Gerta to a city kid I jes met, he said I could borrow her for an hour so's she could stretch her legs 'n have a change of scene. Did ya bring some grain?"

Bug held up the bag. "You mean this is the petting zoo you told me about?"

"Well, Gerta ain't exactly a pettin' zoo, but here, let me show ya what I've got in mind."

Tucking the goose under one arm, Cigar picked up his cane and headed toward the back of the grandstand. Bug followed close behind, pausing to take a bite of her pie. As they rounded the back corner of the grandstand, Nicky Knowlton's shiny black Camaro came into view, parked, just as Walter had said, beneath a large handicapped-parking sign.

"Hey, that car belongs to . . ."

"Shh," Cigar warned. "We have to be quiet — and quick about our business."

The car windows were down. He walked right up to the car and released Gerta, who promptly hopped onto the driver's seat. Then Cigar asked Bug for the grain. Looking around to make sure no one was watching, he tore open the bag, leaned in through the open window and dumped half the contents onto the backseat.

Gerta, who loved her food, flapped between the bucket seats and landed in the back, honking noisily as she began pecking at the food.

"That oughta get the young fella's attention," laughed Cigar as he slipped the bag of leftover grain into his pocket. "The more Gerta eats, the more reminders she'll leave that it ain't nice to play mean tricks on folks."

"Sweet," said Bug, about to finish up her pie. But a hornet buzzed near her mouth, and she hesitated.

"Wait a minute, I want to send this creep a message too," she announced gleefully.

Dipping her fingertips in the gooey pie filling, she quickly printed J-i-r-k across the windshield, dotting the "i" with a small piece of crust.

"I bet the hornets will like that," chortled Bug. "What do you think?"

"I think you spelled it wrong," replied Cigar.

"I sure did," said Bug. "That way, he'll think one of his stupid friends did it."

* * *

Cigar suggested that they give Gerta 20 minutes to make herself at home in Nicky's car, so they slipped back around the corner of the grandstand and headed for the midway.

"I'll give you the grand tour of Tichburg, and you can rest your feet at the same time," said Cigar as they worked their way through the crowd toward the Ferris wheel.

Although there were about a dozen people waiting to get on, Cigar and Bug were motioned to the head of the line and given the first available seat.

When Bug asked Cigar why, he chuckled. "Everybody knows yer busy workin' at The Shoe Pile, 'n they want ya ta enjoy yer breaks."

115

As the Ferris wheel slowly swung upward, Bug got a bird's-eye view of the fairground and the village beyond. For the first time, she could see over the trees that lined the far side of the fairground. The river meandered through the valley as far as she could see, flowing down into the village, dividing it in half. Lined with farms on either side for most of its course, the river was bounded by clusters of houses within the village itself.

"This is the best view you'll get without climbin' the church steeple," said Cigar. "Ya got the whole place spread out before ya from up here."

"Where's Riverview Road?" she asked, remembering the street name the twins' father had called out to her.

Cigar pointed to the right, past the grandstand, to the bridge that carried Main Street over the river. "Just past the bridge," he replied. "It's the nicest spot in Tichburg. I grew up in that big brick house at the far end of the street."

Bug couldn't see the house he was talking about but nodded politely. It was nice to be sitting here, relaxing a bit, and she had to admit that from this height, Tichburg looked to be an OK little place.

The Ferris wheel turned through several rotations, and each time it rose, Cigar pointed out more sights and landmarks. The fire station. The school. Some farms. A couple of churches. But it was the river and the hills sloping upward on either side of it that really impressed her.

"It's pretty, all right," Bug said. "Very quiet and peaceful."

"From up here," Cigar said, "it does have a postcard look to it."

"It's like one of those landscape paintings from a long time ago," said Bug. "Where everything is perfect."

"Not quite perfect, maybe, but pretty nice all the same," Cigar said.

As the Ferris wheel eased them down for the final time, Cigar's voice took on a more serious tone. "Well, girlie, it's time I got Gerta back to Freddie, 'n yer daddy's probably wonderin' where you've gotten to."

Loose Goose

Before returning to The Shoe Pile, Bug just had to have a peek at Nicky's car, so she accompanied Cigar as he made his way along the back of the grandstand. They encountered only a few latecomers who had parked in the field and were walking toward the midway.

But as they drew nearer to the black Camaro, they could see a small knot of people gathered around the car. The driver's door was wide-open, and Nicky Knowlton was reaching into the backseat, trying to grab an enraged, flailing Gerta.

"Whatsa problem?" Cigar asked innocently, as he and Bug approached the car.

"Well, a goose seems to have found its way into that lad's car there," explained a weathered man about Cigar's age.

"And made a considerable mess," added a woman standing beside him. "I can't imagine why the goose would get into the car in the first place."

118

For his part, Nicky was trying desperately to get the bird out of the car, but he was having no luck. Every time he lunged for Gerta, she flapped her huge wings and issued a menacing hiss, driving Nicky back.

Cigar knew that a goose's strong wings can do serious damage during an attack, and he didn't want Nicky or Gerta to get hurt, so he stepped up to the car and offered to help.

"Young fella, if you'd jes step back, I think I can get old Gerta outta yer car."

"Gerta?" shrieked Nicky. "You *know* this goose?"

"Never seen the thing before in my life," Cigar hastily replied. "I call all geese Gerta."

"Look at the mess that stupid bird is making," Nicky shouted, straightening up as he turned to Cigar. "There's poop all over the seats — it'll stink for months."

"That's fer sure," agreed Cigar, nodding wisely. "Now you jes go over there, and I'll see what I can do." He turned and gave Bug a wink as Nicky stormed past her, pushing some of the amused onlookers out of his way. There were a dozen hornets buzzing about the car, and Nicky swatted angrily at them as he walked by.

Cigar motioned for everyone to be quiet, then pulled the bag of grain from his pocket. He started talking quietly to Gerta, placing a handful of grain on the floor of the car in front of the driver's seat. Gerta flapped over the car's console and began to devour the grain. Cigar proceeded to pour a small trail of grain on the ground outside the car that ended in a little pile a few feet away. Then he stood back and waited. After a few moments' hesitation, Gerta hopped out of the car and waddled

119

and pecked her way to the grain that lay by Cigar's feet, honking irritably the whole time. She normally didn't have to work this hard for her feed. As Gerta finished the last few morsels, Cigar bent over and scooped her up.

The small audience applauded Cigar's success. He gave a courtly bow, then turned and headed back to the Loose Goose Bingo with Gerta tucked securely under his arm.

Nicky raced to his car and peered inside. What greeted him was a smelly mixture of goose poop and feathers. Some of the disgusting mess was even smeared on the windows.

At that precise moment, one of the yellow hornets hovering over the sticky "Jirk" printed on the windshield targeted a small, tender portion of Nicky's butt, which was exposed above his low-slung jeans. With an ear-splitting yowl of pain and rage, Nicky erupted backwards from the car, wheeling around and swatting madly at the hornets.

He stopped in mid-swing when he realized there was still a gathering of people watching him. For a split second, Nicky locked eyes with a smiling Bug, then, humiliated and furious, he turned and threw himself into the driver's seat and fired up the engine. He slammed the Camaro into reverse, spinning his tires in the grass as he fled the scene.

Front-Page Famous

By the time Bug rejoined Walter, business had slowed considerably, and she found him sitting on one of the truck's ancient running boards riffling a thick stack of bills. A few customers were quietly picking through the remaining shoes, and Walter was hunched over as discreetly as he could manage, mouthing the growing sum of money by fives and tens.

As Bug approached, he looked up and chuckled with delight, slapping his leg with a fan of money. "Kiddo, we're set for a couple of months. Must be over $3,000 here. Not bad for a day's work." He rolled the bills together, put an elastic around them and stuck the roll in his pocket.

She gave him a little smile, happy for Walter that one of his schemes was finally paying off. She really wanted to tell him how Cigar had taught the bully from the gas station a lesson but then remembered his earlier admonishment that "bullies are best left alone," so she said nothing.

"That means we've sold over half the shoes already," Walter continued. "Sell the rest, we double our money. Those fellows at the diner mentioned a local outdoor market that's open every Wednesday and Saturday, which means in another week, we could . . ."

"Another week!" Bug said incredulously.

"Sure, why not? The word is going to be out about The Shoe Pile after today. We're going to be famous around here. People are going to come looking for us."

"Famous?" Bug hesitated. "Famous how?"

"Well, a lot of people have already bought shoes, and they're going to go home and tell their friends. Then, when the newspaper article and pictures come out . . ."

"What newspaper article?"

"While you were on your break, a newspaper guy came by and interviewed me. I told him all about how we're starting a new life, and he said it's definitely page-one material for *The Wamble Standard*. He took a bunch of pictures, and the story will be in the Wednesday edition. I wanted him to wait around to get a picture of you, but he was in a rush to get over to the poultry judging. He might be back, but he seemed pretty busy."

"Gee, there goes my chance to be famous," teased Bug. "That would have been perfect for my most-embarrassing-moments scrapbook."

She was about to ask Walter whether he had worked out a plan beyond Wednesday when a frail-looking elderly woman tottered up behind her clutching three aerobic shoes to her skinny chest and waving a couple of bills in her free hand.

She thrust the money at Walter and said that she had decided to take two rights and one left.

"There are no more 'lefts' in my size, but I figure I'll just hold on to what I've got until you come back next year."

"Next year?" Bug groaned, but Walter just smiled and nodded. As he escorted the woman clear of the jumble of shoes scattered across the ground, he assured her that next year's shoe pile would make this year's pile look like a molehill.

A baseball game had just ended, and before they could discuss it further, a new influx of customers began drifting toward the pile. Walter removed the roll of money from his pocket and tucked it into the truck's glove compartment, then walked toward the crowd, laughing and hailing a few people heartily as if they were long-lost friends. He had a knack for remembering faces and names, and he was putting his gift to full use here in Tichburg. Some of these were actually earlier customers who were returning with their friends, and in Walter's world, a repeat customer was gold.

Somewhat less enthusiastically, Bug went back to work. Within minutes, she was reaching into the middle of the shrinking pile of shoes to rescue a toddler who had become mired in a knot of laces and soccer boots while his mother was trying on a bright purple sandal.

Return of Frogger

A few minutes later, Frogger sauntered over, wearing his red and green RetroTreds and a sheepish grin. He still had specks of lemon pie filling on his face and shirt.

"Hey," he called to Bug. "How's it going?"

"Oh, it's going all right," she replied. "And so are we, I hope." Bug was longing to put this quirky little village behind her. She was also dreaming of a long soak in a hot bath, followed by a decent meal and a bed to sleep in tonight.

"Have you had a bad day?" Frogger asked.

"Not really, I guess. Except there was this really jerky older kid who gave me a hard time." She described her run-in with Nicky Knowlton but decided, once again, to leave out the part about the goose-poop-and-hornets payback.

"Yeah, I know him," said Frogger sympathetically. "Lives next door to me. He's the meanest kid in Tichburg. My parents have been waiting for him to grow up and leave home ever since he was about 5. If you ignore him, though, he'll leave you alone most of the time."

Walter walked over to them, positively beaming with the sweet smile of success. Sales had been brisk, and from his point of view, Tichburg was golden. He was ready to stay here indefinitely.

"This is one lucky place we've landed," he announced. "We got our grubstake together in a single day, and that's reason enough to think about settling down here for a while."

Bug groaned. "In Tichville?"

"Tich*burg*," Frogger said quietly. "It's called Tichburg."

Bug was staring wide-eyed at Walter. This was *not* what she wanted to hear. Yesterday morning, she had reluctantly abandoned their apartment for the promise of a better life — nice house, great school, good friends, blah, blah, blah. And now, unbelievably, Walter was talking about staying in a dopey little place in the middle of nowhere.

"You can't be serious," she said. "What are we going to do here?"

Meanwhile, Frogger was prattling on about how great Tichburg was. "There's plenty to do. You could go to my school, and I'm sure . . ."

But Bug had tuned him out. She was trying to imagine herself living in Tichburg, with its eccentric residents, half of whom were now wearing unmatched shoes, thanks to Walter and her. Even if there were kids her own age, she would always be known in Tichburg as The Shoe Pile Girl.

Lost in her own gloomy thoughts, she failed to notice the arrival of Cigar Davis, who had drifted over to join the

125

conversation. Bug missed most of what he was saying but was snapped out of her reverie when she heard him giving Walter's plan a ringing endorsement. "You folks'd fit in nicely here. Ya did a whole lot of good fer people today."

Knowing she was powerless to change Walter's mind now, Bug turned and slowly walked away. For the second time that day, she could feel the sting of tears in her eyes. Great, she thought, now I'm turning into a crybaby. She made her way around the empty horse corral, where the barrel races had been run all day, over the racetrack and toward a thick wall of bushes. She didn't know where she was going but just kept walking.

A narrow dirt path led to an opening in the tangled growth, and Bug followed it. It took a sharp turn, then plunged steeply into a small ravine, forcing her to scramble between a pair of gigantic limestone boulders that served as a natural gateway to a sun-dappled woods. The trees were lush, and the space was quiet. It was cooler here, especially after standing in a shadeless field all day, and the noise of the fairground was so faint, Bug was able to block it out.

Continuing along the winding trail, Bug heard the peeping of sparrows as they hopped from tree to tree, tracking her progress through their territory. Out of sight, high overhead, a crow cawed hoarsely. It was peaceful and pretty here, like no place she had ever been before.

She gazed around, taking it all in. Then she heard a soft, murmuring sound. Peering ahead, she saw a clearing around the next bend. As she drew nearer, the gentle murmur became a steady burbling. She stepped out of the shady woods a

126

minute later and found herself standing beside a wide, shallow river, flowing steadily over shelves of limestone.

"Well, if I have to stay here for a while," she announced to the world at large, "this can be my hideout."

Shoe Delivery

"So what now, Walter?" asked Bug.

She had been gone about 30 minutes, and during her absence, the exhibit area had begun to empty out. The pig-guys were dismantling their display, and on the hill, a slow-moving line of cars was exiting the parking field. The Ferris wheel was still turning but was nearly empty. Walter was tossing the remaining shoes into the back of the truck.

"Well, we got an invitation of sorts," Walter announced, bending over to scoop up more merchandise.

He was being vague, which usually indicated that he was up to something, but Bug wasn't about to quiz him. Her walk had improved her mood considerably, and she didn't feel like talking. If Walter wanted to stay in Tichburg for a while, so be it, especially if it meant they'd be out of the shoe business sooner rather than later.

Before he had departed, Cigar had taken Walter aside and

handed him two bowling shoes — women's size nine, one black and orange, the other purple and yellow.

"If you deliver these to the big brick house with the porches, on the corner of Main and Riverview Road, at about 5:30," the old man had said, "I can prett' near guarantee you dinner — maybe even a bed for the night."

"Who lives there?" Walter had asked.

"Sweet lil lady by the name of Dolly Gilmore — Tichburg's fire chief. Best neighbor a fella could ask fer. Jes tell her I bought 'em for her, 'n you're delivering 'em. That'll get us both on her good side. Then, when I show up a few minutes later, I'll ask ya where yer plannin' to spend the night, 'n we'll play it by ear from there."

"Does she have rooms to rent?"

"Not exactly, but she took me in yesterday when I had no place to stay, 'n she's got a couple o' empty rooms that are jes collectin' dust. Besides, when she catches sight of yer young muppet there, her motherly instincts will take over, 'n you'll be in like a pig in a trough."

* * *

At exactly 5:38, Walter pulled the steaming wreck of a truck off Main Street and onto Riverview Road. Wheeling the coughing vehicle to the left, he slowly drove Safely up the sloping driveway of Dolly Gilmore's lovely old brick home. A low stone wall marked the edge of the lawn, and the yard's neat flower beds and tidy vegetable garden bespoke a woman who prided herself on running a meticulous household.

"Why are we stopping here?" asked Bug, who had said little while they were packing up at the fairground.

"Old Cigar asked me to drop off some bowling shoes to a friend of his."

The truck jolted forward and died, then started to roll backward. Walter quickly set the parking brake, and the truck groaned to a stop. He grabbed the bowling shoes and motioned for Bug to follow him.

"I'll wait here," she said. "I'm tired and stinky."

"So am I, Bug, but Cigar would like us to meet this Mrs. Gilmore. She's the fire chief. A *woman* fire chief. A pretty progressive place, this Tichburg."

"Should we bring the money with us?" Bug asked, pointing to the battered glove compartment.

"Too big a roll for that," he replied. "It's hard to sit and be sociable if you've got a wad of bills the size of a turnip stuck in your pocket. It'll be fine where it is."

"I hope so. I'd hate to have it stolen after what we went through to get it."

Just then, a short, stout, pleasant-looking woman stepped out onto the side porch of the sprawling house and looked down at them from the top of the steps. She was wearing an apron, which she wiped her hands on as she stood there, puzzling over why a beat-up old dump truck had just parked in her driveway.

"C'mon, Bug, it's time to meet Mrs. Dolly Gilmore." Walter climbed down from the truck, holding the door open for Bug to follow. "And mind your manners."

* * *

"Good afternoon, ma'am," boomed Walter as he walked up to the house. "I'm guessing you'd be Mrs. Dolly Gilmore."

130

She nodded, curious about the stranger striding toward her wearing baggy shorts and what appeared to be one red and one orange slipper.

"The name is Walter Hapensak, Mrs. Gilmore, and this is my daughter Bug." He motioned behind him, pausing for a second to give Bug a chance to speak, but she remained silent, so he continued.

"Your friend Cigar Davis asked me to drop off these shoes on our way out of Tichburg. He had to go into town."

Walter climbed halfway up the steps and handed Mrs. Gilmore the brightly colored shoes. She took them politely, one in each hand, and examined them carefully.

"They look like bowling shoes," she said hesitantly.

"That would be correct," said Walter. "Genuine Pro-Bowl Strikers. Size nine." He glanced at her feet quickly to confirm that Cigar had made an accurate assessment of her size. "You could try them on while we wait, and if they don't fit, we'll get you a pair that does."

"Bowling shoes?"

"Yes. Cigar told me you're quite an expert at the game."

Mrs. Gilmore's cautious mouth broke into a wide smile.

"That man is truly living in the past. My word! I haven't bowled in a hen's age. In fact, the bowling alley in Wamble burned down over 10 years ago."

This caught Walter off guard. Mrs. Gilmore passed the shoes back and brushed her hands across the wide expanse of apron.

"It was kind of you to stop by," she said. "Now, if you'll excuse me, I've got dinner in the oven, and I'd best get back to it before it burns. I'll tell Mr. Davis you were by and explain to him that I'm 70 years old and don't bend and slide the way I used to. That man is a character." She chuckled and turned to go.

Walter glanced at his watch and wondered where Cigar was. If their plan was going to work, Walter would have to stall for time.

"Could I impose on you for a small favor?" he improvised. "We've been down at the fair all day, standing in a hot, dusty field selling these shoes, and I wonder whether my daughter Bug could freshen up in your bathroom."

He glanced at Bug, who was standing beside the truck, shooting her a look that implored her to take advantage of any hospitality Mrs. Gilmore might offer. Bug crossed her eyes at him in response, then turned to Mrs. Gilmore, smiled somewhat sweetly and said, "The restrooms in the park were pretty stinky, and I . . ."

But Dolly Gilmore cut her off. "No need to explain, dear. Come right in. We ladies need our running water."

They both followed Mrs. Gilmore as she hobbled into the kitchen, directing Bug down a hallway to the bathroom, while motioning for Walter to have a seat on an antique wooden chair. The kitchen was fragrant with the delectable smell of fresh-baked bread, which was cooling on the table beside Walter, and another enticing aroma was coming from the stove. Excusing herself, Mrs. Gilmore swung open the oven door to inspect a large, golden-skinned chicken bubbling in a roasting pan.

132

Dog Fight

When Bug returned to the kitchen a few minutes later, Walter was chatting amiably to the fire chief, offering her advice on shoes. He was recommending a pair of walking shoes that might give her some relief from an unspecified foot ailment. His face brightened as his daughter entered the room.

"Bug, I'm sure we've got a good supply of those two-tone CloudWalkers. Would you please climb up into the truck and dig out a pair of size nines? I'm sure Mrs. Gilmore would find them a great improvement. And keep an eye peeled for some of those RiverStalker hiking sandals too. They were really popular today. Everyone was raving about how comfortable they are. And the straps are extra-wide, really soft and super-strong too."

Mrs. Gilmore protested, but Walter assured her it was no problem. Happy not to be drawn into yet another conversation about shoes, Bug hurried outside. As she skipped down the

133

steps, however, she thought she spotted some movement at the back of the truck. Jumping off the fourth step, she raced behind the truck and caught a fleeting glimpse of Nicky Knowlton bounding across Mrs. Gilmore's lawn, then clambering awkwardly over the low stone wall into the yard next door. A few seconds later, she heard a door slam and guessed that he had escaped to his own house, probably with an armful of stolen shoes.

Bug decided it wasn't worth causing a fuss over a few unmatched shoes, especially in view of the "message" she and Cigar had sent Nicky with the help of Gerta the goose. Then she remembered the $3,000 Walter had stashed in the glove compartment. Her heart pounding in fear, she scrambled into the cab. At first, the compartment door would not open. She slammed it a few times with the heel of her hand, and it suddenly fell forward, revealing the thick roll of cash right where Walter had left it.

Heaving a huge sigh of relief, Bug crammed an old rag around the money so that it couldn't be seen, then pushed the small door closed, but it refused to stay shut. Exasperated, she finally gave up and slid back across the seat to fetch the shoes for Mrs. Gilmore. When that chore was done, they could find someplace to spend the night and enjoy a good dinner. They certainly deserved it.

For the first time since they'd driven out of the city, Bug was feeling clean. In the bathroom, she had washed her hands and arms, her face and neck and around her ears. She had even taken the liberty of brushing her hair with one of Mrs. Gilmore's brushes. So it was with some regret that she

134

climbed up the side of the dusty truck, peeled back the tarpaulin and dropped down into the shoes. She was sick of being tired and dirty and hungry. But she knew that what stood between her and a warm bath was a pair of shoes for the fire chief, so she set to work.

Bug spotted a size-nine, lilac and gray, left CloudWalker within minutes but had less luck finding a suitably sized mate. Although she found several righties, they were all the wrong size. Realizing she did not know for sure that Mrs. Gilmore was a size nine, she started a small pile of walking shoes in other sizes as well. In 10 minutes, Bug had sifted through half the pile and still had not come up with a CloudWalker size nine right, so she decided it was time to pull off the tarpaulin completely. It was drooping down into the pile, and every time she moved, she had to wrestle it to one side. Although it would take a considerable amount of effort to retie it across the load, there seemed no alternative.

Releasing the ropes at the front of the dumper on both sides, Bug slowly rolled the huge piece of blue plastic toward the back of the truck and balanced it on the heavy steel tailgate. Then she returned to work, kneeling down and methodically grabbing shoes and pitching them forward to join the pile she had already inspected.

Within minutes, she had dug out a pair of the RiverStalker hiking sandals Walter had suggested. She decided to keep the likely prospects separate from the rest and tossed the sandals out the back of the truck, then picked up the half-dozen CloudWalkers she had set aside and threw them onto the grass as well.

"Almost done," she thought to herself. "Just have to find a CloudWalker size nine rightie, and we'll be out of here." But Bug had not counted on Barney, a playful, rambunctious beagle that lived a few houses down the street.

Having escaped the confines of the porch where he usually spent the day, Barney was enjoying a late-afternoon stroll down Riverview Road when he saw several running shoes come flying out the back of a dump truck and bounce onto Mrs. Gilmore's lawn.

Barney dashed up to the truck and caught a left-footed, size-nine CloudWalker on its second bounce. He may have intended to take it back to his porch three houses away, but the sight of an enraged girl bursting from the back of the truck inspired him to turn the whole thing into an exciting game of Catch-Me-If-You-Can. Leaning sharply to the right, he started tearing circles around the truck, spurred on by the girl's shouts.

Bug was furious. No way was she going to crawl through that pile again in search of another left-footed CloudWalker all because of an ornery little canine. In frustration, she picked up a hiking boot and hurled it as the dog raced by, still clutching the walking shoe in its mouth. The beagle easily dodged the missile and disappeared behind the front bumper, ready to start another lap.

If she were going to recover the shoe, Bug knew she would have to wage the battle at ground level. But as she kicked one leg over the side of the truck to climb down, her ankle got caught in one of the tie-down ropes attached to the tarpaulin. Her patience at an end and close to tears once

136

more, she threw herself down onto the pile of shoes and struggled to unwrap the rope. She was so tired, she couldn't concentrate and only managed to tighten its hold on her leg.

At that precise moment, the ancient truck gave a slight shudder that Bug barely noticed. In fact, not until the second or third such tremor did she realize something was terribly wrong. Struggling to her feet, still entangled in the rope, Bug looked over the side of the truck. The beagle, gripping the shoe tightly in its mouth, was looking up at her. Barney was not moving, but Safely was. With each shudder, the truck rolled backwards a little bit more, and by the fourth groan, it began picking up speed and was coming ever closer to the street.

In imminent danger, Bug frantically tried to climb out but was held fast by the snarled rope. As the truck rolled to the end of the driveway and bounced across the sidewalk, she desperately clawed at the rope. She finally managed to pull her ankle free as the truck sped across the street and began accelerating down the steep slope that led to the river. Before Bug could even call out for help, the truck hurtled over the edge of the riverbank.

Crash, Splash and Thrash

For miles upstream, the river meandered gently through the countryside, but in Tichburg, it narrowed and became a torrent that rushed down through a series of rocky rapids. With a humongous *ker-sploosh*, the old truck hit the water hard, dumping its cargo of shoes, boxes and Bug into the cold, fast-moving current.

The blue tarpaulin attached to the truck billowed to the surface like an open parachute and threatened to trap Bug within its bulk, holding her down as it slowly filled with water. She kicked and thrashed her legs to push herself away from it. Then, in a sudden whoosh, the tarpaulin disappeared beneath the surface, dragged down as the truck sank to the bottom. Bug wasn't a strong swimmer, and the current was pulling hard as the water rushed toward the old mill dam.

For more than a century, the dam had funneled water past a huge stone flour mill, which was now just an attractive ruin.

On the far side of the river, water cascaded over the dam into a deep swimming hole. But on the near side, the dam had been built higher to force water through a submerged chute that acted like a gigantic water cannon, spewing out a powerful, roaring jet of frothing water which plunged to the rocks below. For years, parents had warned their children to stay well away from the dam. Since the old mill raceways had been removed, the undertow and the whirlpool created by the chute were deadly.

Bug fought desperately to escape the pull of the current. She had seen enough adventure films to know that water moving this quickly was usually on its way over something high and dangerous. But when she tried to swim, her left arm felt numb and useless. Something was very wrong. The final slam of the truck must have done some serious damage.

Bobbing up and down and gasping for air as she was dragged along, Bug tried to remain level-headed and assess her situation. Occasionally, submerged rocks banged and scraped her legs. To her left, she could see a jumble of limestone slabs jutting into the water from the steep bank. With a herculean effort, she kicked her battered legs and stroked lopsidedly with her right arm in a frantic attempt to reach the limestone shelf.

When her fingers slammed into the limestone, she cried out in pain but instinctively gripped the slippery rock and held fast. She tried to pull herself onto the limestone, but there was no place for her feet to get hold, and without the use of her left arm, she couldn't manage it. She clung to the rock with one hand, exhausted. The relentless pull of the river and the cold water were draining her last bit of energy.

Bug was close to giving up and simply letting the river carry her away when she became aware of a series of sharp barks. As the only witness to the accident, Barney had raced along the riverbank, following as Bug was swept downstream. He now charged through the underbrush and leaped from the shore to the shelf of limestone that led to Bug. Undeterred by the slippery footing, Barney made his way to the edge of the limestone and barked triumphantly.

* * *

"Good boy," murmured Bug, forgetting that she had been throwing shoes at him only moments before. "I need help. I can't hold on much longer."

All around her, shoes bobbed and eddied about in the water. Some plummeted over the dam, while others were sucked into the vortex that would propel them through the underbelly of the ruin. Several had become trapped in the protected niche of the limestone shelf, and it was one of those that Barney retrieved. Gripping a neon-blue RiverStalker hiking sandal in his teeth, he carried it over to Bug and lay down close to her hand.

Thinking the beagle wanted to play, Bug felt a wave of hopelessness. Then she wondered whether he was actually offering her a lifeline. For a fleeting moment, she was torn by indecision. If she let go of the rock, she was afraid she would be caught up in the current. But when Barney inched forward on his belly, whimpering, she decided to put her faith in the little dog. She took a deep breath to calm herself, then released her hold on the rock and grasped at the wide strap of the sandal.

140

As her fingers closed over the strap, Barney's jaws clamped tightly onto the sandal, and he slipped and scrambled backwards along the shelf. Bug kicked with all her might. Slowly, with Barney's help, she was able to drag herself out of the river onto the limestone shelf.

Coughing up water and moaning in pain, Bug managed to roll onto her back. She closed her eyes as she felt the warm late-afternoon sun on her face. Then everything went black.

Waking Up

The next day was Sunday, a fact that slowly registered with Bug as she recognized the deep DING, DING, DING of a far-off church bell. She opened her eyes and looked around.

She found herself lying in a comfortable bed in a sunny bedroom decorated in cheerful pinks and yellows. The early-morning sun streaming through the open window seemed to illuminate the sheer yellow curtains. Old-fashioned pink and cream wallpaper strewn with bouquets of delicately entwined roses adorned the walls. A small yellow desk and matching chair stood in the corner, surrounded by white bookshelves filled with a hundred or more books, all neatly upright, their spines facing out. The wide floorboards had been painted an eggshell white, although they were visible only around the edges of a thick, knotted rag rug that had been crafted in a dozen shades of blue and yellow. Remembering the gloomy bedroom she had left behind in the city just two days ago,

142

Bug thought this was the prettiest room she had ever seen.

At first, she didn't know where she was and suspected she might be dreaming. But as she continued to look around, she began to recall the events of the previous day — a day that had been so busy and full, in fact, that it seemed weeks long.

The window was right beside the bed, and Bug could see the branches of the big trees growing in the side yard. A gentle breeze riffled the curtains, and the air was sweet and fresh-smelling. Birds were chirping, and off in the distance, she could hear a dog barking and the resonant tones of the ringing bell.

As she raised her head to have a better look, she became aware of her sore, aching body. Her left arm was cradled in a sling that held it snugly against her chest, and when she moved, her shoulder throbbed painfully. Below the crisp, white sheets, she could feel a dull weariness in her legs.

Kicking free of the sheets, she rolled her legs over the side of the high bed and slowly sat up. She was wearing a beautifully embroidered cotton nightgown that was a bit big. A mirror on the back of the door allowed her a glimpse of herself. Her hair hung limply around her face. There was a small bandage high on her forehead, and her right cheek was scraped and raw-looking. Her free arm had several large bruises on it, and her hand was slightly swollen and sore.

* * *

As Bug was assessing her injuries and her whereabouts, there was a light tap on the door, and Mrs. Gilmore peeked in.

"I thought I heard you moving around, dear," she said softly. "May I come in?" Bug nodded, and Mrs. Gilmore slipped into the room. Smiling, she laid her hand gently on Bug's forehead, checking for a fever. She idly brushed the hair away from Bug's face with her fingers.

"My word! You had us scared to death yesterday. We found you lying down there on the rocks by the river looking half dead. I don't know how you managed to pull yourself out of the water with a broken collarbone and such, but it was a blessing."

"There was a dog," said Bug. "It pulled me out."

"What kind of dog, dear?" asked Mrs. Gilmore.

"A little brown and white dog. When I was in the back of the truck looking for a CloudWalker, it started grabbing shoes and running off with them, but after the crash, it came to help me."

"Why, that sounds like Barney," Mrs. Gilmore said thoughtfully. "He's always getting loose and making a nuisance of himself when the McAvoys go out. I'm constantly shooing him away from my garden. Well, he's certainly redeemed himself now." She smiled warmly at Bug.

"Where's Walter?" queried Bug.

"Oh, I stuck him in the room behind the kitchen with Cigar Davis. Cigar drifted back into Tichburg a couple days ago. He had no place to stay, so I gave him a room until he gets settled. He and your dad are like a couple of overgrown kids back there. They're sleeping on bunk beds, if you can believe it."

Picturing her father climbing into the top bunk brought a smile to Bug's face.

Then she suddenly remembered how she had ended up in the river. "Is the truck going to be all right?"

144

"Well, it's still underwater, but the boys on the rescue and recovery team are coming back this morning with Jake Hartington's big tow truck, and they're going to try winching it out. I doubt it will ever run again, but you just can't leave a dump truck in the river."

Bug nodded silently in agreement, wondering whether the big wad of money was still stowed in the glove compartment.

Breakfast at Dolly's

Before breakfast, Bug finally got to take the bath she had been longing for the previous afternoon. After running the bathwater into the old cast-iron tub, Mrs. Gilmore sprinkled in some lavender bath salts, helped remove Bug's sling and told her to have a good long soak before coming downstairs. She then laid out a plush bath towel and a matching bathrobe for Bug before leaving the room.

An hour later, Bug gingerly made her way downstairs, holding her left arm across her chest to keep the weight off her broken collarbone. As she entered the kitchen, she was greeted heartily by Walter and Cigar, who both rose to their feet and hugged her gently. Across the kitchen, Mrs. Gilmore was busily attending to a small pot of oatmeal on the stove and told the men to let the poor girl sit. Seeing the sling in Bug's hand, she turned off the burner, bustled over and eased Bug's arm back into a comfortable position in the sling.

"The doctor says it will be about a week before your collarbone starts to mend," explained Mrs. Gilmore. "The sling just helps hold everything in place while it's healing. All you have to do in the meantime is take life easy."

As Bug was being served her bowl of oatmeal and slices of fresh toast, there was a knock on the screen door, then Frogger stepped into the kitchen bursting with news.

"Jake Hartington is here with his tow truck. Joe Huffman's going to dive underwater to attach some cables to the truck. And they're blocking off the street and using your driveway as the anchor point. Randy Timmerman is bringing in Rollie Estabrook's backhoe but says they might need a couple more trucks from Wamble because the dump truck's so heavy."

He paused to catch his breath and, looking beyond Mrs. Gilmore, spotted Bug. "Hey, how are you feeling?"

Bug gave a little shrug to indicate she was all right, probably.

"Well, I've got to get back to the street. I'm keeping traffic moving so everyone's got room to work. See you later."

Picking up their coffee cups, Cigar and Walter followed the boy outside, leaving Bug to finish her breakfast while Mrs. Gilmore filled the sink with hot water.

"I'd better slip down there just to make sure everything's all right. I don't think this is official fire department business anymore, but a lot of the fellows are going to be helping out, and it wouldn't do not to have the chief check in."

She chuckled to herself as she turned off the water and began slipping dishes into the sink.

"Now yesterday's rescue, *that* was department business.

147

The boys did a grand job hauling you up that steep bank. Got to use the backboard and all their lines. We haven't had a river rescue in about three years, and they came through with flying colors."

Bug had a vague recollection of being strapped to the board and eventually lifted into a waiting ambulance. The ambulance was old and more like a truck, with just enough room for a skinny stretcher. In fact, it was the ambulance she'd seen at the fairground yesterday after the accident with Mrs. Troth and the twins.

"I don't remember a lot about that," she confessed. "But there was one man who kept saying really funny things while they were carrying me up — he was nice, in a goofy sort of way."

"Now that would be Randy, Tichburg's biggest kid. He's Doc Timmerman's son. Good firefighter and medic but a real nut. He was the one who drove you to the hospital."

Bug had a clearer memory of the hospital. It had been so white and bright. She had spent the whole time there lying on her back with people peering down at her. Walter had been beside her constantly, looking worried.

"The doctor in Wamble says you're lucky to be alive. Claims you must be made of rubber to have gotten only a bit banged up. He says a broken collarbone in an accident like that hardly counts."

"I guess we lost everything in the truck," Bug said.

"Oh, dear, I'm afraid so. The river is full of floating shoes. They'll be fishing them out at Wamble for the next three weeks, I'm sure."

"There were boxes too. All the stuff from our apartment

148

— everything we own. My clothes and books. The kitchen stuff. Some photo albums." At the thought of the photo albums, Bug's heart sank. They contained the only pictures she had of her mother, all the snapshots of baby Bug sitting on her knee. Picnics. Christmas dinners. Birthdays.

"Oh, my, yes. But don't worry, people will bring what they find back here, and I'm sure we'll be able to salvage some of it. But you're certainly going to need clothes. I still have some of my daughter's things in your room. We can sort through them later. Right now, though, I had better go see how they're doing out there."

After Bug finished her porridge and drained her second glass of orange juice, she put her dishes into the sink and wandered out the kitchen door. It opened onto a side porch, which connected to a big front veranda that overlooked the street and the river. Below her lay a scene of organized chaos. A police cruiser was parked across Riverview Road to block traffic, its lights flashing to indicate that there was a serious situation in Tichburg which warranted official intervention. A police officer was leaning against the car sipping coffee from a Styrofoam cup, while Frogger stood out on Main Street, highly visible in a fluorescent orange vest and his red and green RetroTred Hoopsters, waving traffic past the intersection.

At the end of the driveway, the action was more intense. Three vehicles were backed up near the edge of the riverbank — a large tow truck with its bar of yellow warning lights blinking urgently, a rusty backhoe and a huge red farm tractor with gargantuan double rear wheels. People were clustered all around them, watching the action intently and pointing at the river where the old dump truck had settled. Children ran from group to group at knee level, darting in and out, barely listening to the adults, who occasionally warned them away from the various cables and chains that led down to the river. Beside the tow truck, Mrs. Gilmore was conferring with a half-dozen men, alternately pointing and nodding her head as she discussed their plan.

After a while, a short man wearing a wet suit pulled himself out of the water, removed his flippers and diver's mask and made his way up the riverbank. He walked over to where Walter and Cigar were standing and paused briefly, shaking his head in response to something Walter had said. Bug imagined he had asked the diver whether he had seen the roll of money. The answer seemed to be no.

Then the diver joined the group gathered around Mrs. Gilmore. Bug could tell by his hand motions that the truck was now attached to the tow cables. The recovery operation was about to begin.

Truck Recovery

Bug watched anxiously, hoping that by some miracle, their $3,000 had not been swept down the river and lost forever. She sat down on a creaky porch swing that graced one end of the veranda and moved gently back and forth as the drama unfolded before her.

She was so intent on the action across the street that she didn't notice Barney the beagle had climbed the porch steps to join her until he nudged her leg with his cold, wet nose. He jumped up onto the swing and sat beside her. Bug patted his head, and the two of them sat there in companionable silence, enjoying a bond that had been forged from a near tragedy. Ten minutes later, Safely — the dump truck that had been part of Walter's master plan for their new life — was hauled from the river, battered and waterlogged.

* * *

By noon, Mrs. Gilmore had sorted through her daughter's

151

old clothes and picked out a couple of dresses and some underwear for Bug. Her daughter Jeanette was married now and lived halfway across the country, but luckily, chirped Mrs. Gilmore, the style of simple summer dresses had not changed much over the past three decades. Bug seldom wore dresses and never followed fashion, but she smiled politely and chose a sleeveless blue denim shift with a peace sign embroidered on it. It buttoned up in front, which made it easy to put on around her injured arm.

Returning to the kitchen, Bug found Cigar making coffee, singing a little ditty about a peg-legged pirate named Barrett. At the table, Walter was fiddling with a pen and paper, adding columns of numbers and scribbling notes. Near at hand were some sodden papers relating to the ownership and insurance of the ruined truck and an official-looking document.

"What's all that?" Bug asked.

"Nothing much. Just some paperwork that has to be filled out when a truck takes a tumble in the river."

Bug picked it up and started to read: "Fresh Water Branch. Department of the Environment. You are hereby charged with breach of Section III of the . . ."

"I'll save you the trouble of straining your eyes reading the small print," Walter laughed. "They're charging me with polluting the river and say I'll have to pay for the cleanup."

"How much did it cost to get the truck out?"

"Now that wuz free, o' course," piped up Cigar. "All those folks donated their time — except for Fred Keeling. He's a police officer and has to charge the county overtime for weekend incidents of this sort."

152

"Then what's to pay?" demanded Bug.

"Well, I guess the issue is the 400 to 500 shoes floating downstream," said Walter. "Seems there are laws about that sort of thing. If they stick it to us, we'll have to pay a hefty fine in addition to the cost of the cleanup."

"Ridiculous," snorted Cigar. "Too much regulation these days when a fella can't even afford to have an accident."

"Well, the investigator and Officer Keeling say it was a preventable accident. They checked the truck before it was towed away, and the parking brake wasn't set. I was sure I'd put it on when we parked in the driveway. But I saw it myself. It wasn't on . . . just a real dumb mistake on my part."

"You *didn't* forget," thundered Bug, surprising everyone with the vehemence in her voice. "It was that jerk with the black Camaro. I saw him sneaking away from the truck when I went outside to look for those shoes for Mrs. Gilmore. He must have deliberately released the brake."

"Whoa. Hold on a minute," cautioned Walter. "That's a very serious accusation to make about someone we don't even know. It's the kind of thing that can lead to a lot of trouble. Besides, it doesn't make any sense. We've never done anything to him. Why would he do such a horrible thing to us?"

"I don't know," said Bug flatly, fearing that she and Cigar had triggered this whole terrible incident by turning Gerta the goose loose in Nicky's car. She glanced over at Cigar, and he looked away.

Meeting the Neighbors

The thought that Nicky Knowlton may have sabotaged Safely in retaliation for the goose in his car weighed heavily on Bug's mind, but she had no time to fret about it.

As if by some secret signal, people started arriving in Mrs. Gilmore's kitchen shortly after noon, loaded down with platters of sandwiches and desserts, salads and cold cuts. The kitchen quickly filled up with people and food, and Mrs. Gilmore shooed everyone out onto the porch, then phoned the fire station and asked Randy Timmerman to bring over some tables and chairs from the community hall.

It was a lovely late-August day, not too hot or humid, and within half an hour, six long tables and dozens of chairs had been set up on the lawn.

Frogger arrived, accompanied by Barney, who proudly trotted across the yard sporting a red ribbon on his collar. Mrs. Gilmore asked Frogger to take Bug outside and introduce her to the neighbors. Everyone wanted to say hello, and it wouldn't do to have her sit inside by herself. Bug offered a feeble protest, but Mrs. Gilmore would hear none of it.

"These folks are concerned about you and have gone to a great deal of trouble for you and your father since last night. All they ask in return is to be able to take a close look at you to be sure you're really all right. Everyone's friendly, so you needn't feel shy."

Frogger steered Bug out onto the porch and around the corner to the swing. "It's hard to say no to Mrs. Gilmore," he explained. "She always knows what should be done."

For the next hour, Frogger introduced Bug to the entire population of 473 Tichburgers — or so it seemed to Bug. Many of them happily pointed out that they were wearing the shoes she or Walter had sold them at the fairground. Others, dressed in their Sunday best, had stopped by on their way home from church. Most of the children were fussing over Barney and offering him dog treats. He was wagging his tail joyously, lapping up the attention.

Bug was convinced that she would never learn all these people's names, even if she and Walter were to stay here for years. In the city, they had been surrounded by strangers, and names were not important, but here in Tichburg, every face had a name and, if Frogger were to be believed, a story or two to tell.

"That's Birdie Pickett," he said, pointing to a petite, neatly dressed, elderly woman wearing huge, round glasses that made her look like an owl. "She owns the Lucky Dollar store and lives in back of it. My parents say the store is full of mice, and they won't let me buy any candy from the bulk-food section because it might have mouse poop in it.

"And there's Mrs. Codger. She runs the retirement home. Everyone calls the people who live there Codger's Lodgers." Frogger lowered his voice to a whisper. "They say she has this room in the basement, and when someone dies of old age, she puts the body there until the funeral home can pick it up. Once she forgot about one, and it stayed there for three weeks, until someone noticed the old guy hadn't been to the dining room for a while."

A seemingly endless line of well-wishers hugged Bug, patted her on the back, tweaked her cheeks and congratulated her on surviving such an ordeal. From time to time, she saw people talking earnestly with Cigar, then passing him envelopes before moving on.

At the first opportunity, she excused herself and scurried into the house, hoping to find a quiet place so that she could get her thoughts together. What she found, instead, was wall-to-wall people chatting in the kitchen. As she was trying to get to the stairs to go hide out in her room, she was waylaid by Ken Bartlett, a one-footed man who, she remembered, had purchased several left shoes yesterday.

It seemed that he had had a similar accident at about her age, having fallen off the dam into a log chute, where he had suffered a badly broken arm, several cracked ribs and a shattered kneecap. "I had to give up my dream of becoming a professional bowler," he confessed. "I became a barber instead. Retired now, of course. Did you know that barbers are the most respected people in the world?"

"They are?" responded Bug.

"Indeed, they are," grinned Ken. "Men always take off their hats to barbers!"

With that, the old fellow burst into such a fit of laughter that his false teeth almost flew out of his mouth. "Do you get it?" he gasped. "They take off their . . ."

"Yes, sir," smiled Bug politely. "That's a good one." Then she excused herself and made her way back to the kitchen.

Treasure Revealed

Squeezing her way through the throng of people in the kitchen, Bug reached the door of the room her father was sharing with Cigar and slipped inside. Judging from the furniture and contents, this bedroom had once belonged to someone who loved sports.

While it may have started out as a mere bedroom, it had become a sports museum. Trophies lined the bookshelves, and the walls were covered with posters of sports heroes whose glory years had long come and gone. Hockey players smiled down beside swinging batters. Helmeted football greats glared fiercely out at leaping basketball players. The bedspreads on the bunk beds were endorsed by the National Hockey League, the pillows were adorned with Red Wings and Maple Leafs logos. There were baseball caps and gloves and a football helmet emblazoned with the name Wamble Warriors.

Bug was examining a picture frame filled with photographs of a boy in a variety of sports uniforms when the door swung open and Cigar entered the room.

She started to explain her presence in his room, but he just shushed her.

"No need ta explain," he said, as he sat down on the lower bunk. "Too many people out there fer me too."

Turning back to the photographs, Bug asked, "Is this Mrs. Gilmore's son?" She studied the pictures some more. At 3, he was on skates. At 5, he was playing baseball. At 15, he was a football hero surrounded by smiling cheerleaders.

"Yep, that was Terry Gilmore, greatest junior athlete Tichburg ever produced. His mother's pride 'n joy. Won all the ribbons 'n trophies there were ta be won around these parts by the time he wuz 17. If he wuz alive today, he'd be 45 or so — probably some sort of sports commentator or maybe a high school coach, with bad knees 'n great memories."

"What happened to him?"

"Died in a car accident a long time ago. Bad luck, really. He wuz waitin' fer a ride home from Wamble after a school football practice. Dolly was late pickin' him up, so he caught a lift with some kids headin' back ta Tichburg. They were drivin' too fast 'n ran off the road. Three of the kids walked away from the crash, but Terry died on the spot."

"That's awful."

"Yep, it is. That's why there are so many folks out there today celebratin' the fact that yer still alive. It's a fine line between good luck 'n bad luck, 'n you seem to have the best kind. You must'a thought you were about to go over Niagara

159

Falls when you bounced down that hill and got dumped into the river. Ya could've been a goner about 10 different ways, but ya got yerself hauled out by a mutt everyone's been complainin' about fer years."

"Yes, I'm all right, but I wouldn't exactly say we've had good luck. We lost all our money and everything we own. Our truck just got towed to the wrecking yard. Now they're going to fine us for polluting the river and make us pay for cleaning up a mess that wasn't really our fault."

"That may well be true, young lady," said Cigar, "but there's a whole lotta folks out there who took a likin' ta you 'n yer daddy yesterday. And there's been a steady stream of 'em droppin' by all day ta offer their support — not ta mention all that good food. And, best of all, ya met me." He chuckled good-naturedly.

"Well," Bug replied, "you've been really nice to me and everything, but I keep thinking if we hadn't stuck that goose in the back of Nicky's car yesterday, none of this would have happened."

"True nuff, 'n I accept full responsibility fer that. I admit I've got some debts ta pay, 'n not just ta you 'n yer daddy."

Cigar bent down and hauled an old biscuit tin and a small cigar box out from under the bed and set them next to him.

"Day before yesterday, I got young Frogger to retrieve these from the house where I grew up. Jes down at the end of the street there. Rich couple o' city folks 'n their two wild scamps live there now."

"The Troth twins?" interrupted Bug, remembering the two little terrors in the sheep pen.

"That's right. Like two peas in a pod. Anyway, Frogger crawled around in that attic fer me 'n recovered a couple o' things I left there a dog's age ago — stuff I started collectin' when I wuz a kid nearly yer age, I suppose."

He removed the lid of the biscuit tin to reveal a half-dozen painted lead soldiers in a variety of battle stances, medals from an army uniform, a jackknife, an assortment of old coins, some paper money, and a pocket watch. He picked up the knife and weighed it in the palm of his hand.

"My daddy gave me this when I turned 10. Gave me the watch when I wuz 14. He wuz a pretty formal fella, my daddy. Always presentin' stuff to me 'n my sister on our birthdays. I liked the knife fine but rarely bothered with the watch. Gettin' places on time didn't seem to matter much in those days. Hardly used it, which that lawyer fella, Mel Dobbins, sez probably makes it more valuable, cuz I never wore it out. He also sez there's plenty o' collectors out there who'd pay a pretty penny for these little Civil War soldiers and my granddaddy's old war medals, though I don't know as I'd part with 'em. And he's callin' in some expert to have a look at my coins.

"Anyway, when I turned 18, Daddy gave me a bunch o' stock certificates. It was the Depression then, 'n a lot o' companies had gone broke, 'n a lot more weren't worth too much. But he told me to hold on to 'em as long as I could, cuz one day, I might need something real bad, 'n then I could sell 'em."

"And did you?"

"Never seemed to need anything that bad. And to tell ya

161

the truth, I forgot about 'em till Frogger handed these boxes back ta me. Well, I mentioned those stock certificates, kinda casual-like, to the bank manager at the fair yesterday, and he prett' near did a jig by the pie tent. He insisted I bring 'em to the bank right away. Drove me over to Dolly's to pick 'em up, then opened the bank jes fer me. I coulda waited till Monday, but he was fairly bustin' at the seams to see them certificates.

"Turns out most of the certificates my daddy gave me over the years are worthless, but a few are from companies that're still in business. It seems they've grown like Topsy, and that bank manager sez I'm a pretty wealthy fella right now."

"Take it from me, Cigar," warned Bug, "and put those things in a safe place. Right now, our hard-earned $3,000 is probably feeding the fish on the other side of the dam."

"Don't ya worry none. All that paper, good 'n bad, is sittin' in the vault at the bank in Wamble right now. Next week, that banker 'n Mel Dobbins are settin' off on a lil adventure of their own to find out jes how rich I am. I figger there'll be enough to replace your shoe money and more to spare."

"You'd do that for us?" said Bug quietly.

"Well, o' course. Maybe even a bit more — kind of a loan till ya get back on yer feet. You 'n yer daddy are the sort of people we need around here, 'n I'm not the only one who thinks so. All those folks out there today have been bringin' donations to help pay for the cleanup and the fine. 'N we'd be real happy if ya decide to stay around these parts fer a spell."

Bug could feel her eyes welling up with tears and threw

162

her good arm around Cigar's neck and hugged him tightly. "Gosh, thanks," she said. Then, embarrassed by her show of emotion, she pulled back and began fussing self-consciously with her hair.

"Me 'n yer daddy have already had a word about this," said Cigar. "'N I want ya ta talk ta Frogger 'bout signing up fer school. Starts next Tuesday, ya know."

Laundered Money

Outside, a group of people had gathered around Walter, who was gesturing excitedly and explaining that tourists would come a long way to experience life in a small village like Tichburg.

"This whole community of yours is like a yesteryear theme park, but it's authentic. There's got to be a way to package this to share with the rest of the world. People would pay to spend a day here. Why, you could have a church supper every night of the week. Beans on Monday. Chicken on Tuesday . . ."

"Ham supper on Wednesday," offered Harold Kingsley, the retired postmaster.

"Oh, no, ham's much better later in the week," argued Birdie Pickett, who seemed to have a contrary opinion on most matters. "I'd have Mrs. Codger's delightful tuna casserole on Wednesday, then ham on Thursday and a fish fry every Friday."

"Oh, boy," roared Walter. "Fish Fridays. Fantastic! I love it! Love it! Love it!"

Bug was watching Walter in action from the porch. The main crowd was finally thinning out as the citizens of Tichburg headed home to resume their Sunday routines. In the side yard, Frogger and Randy Timmerman were busy hanging dozens — maybe even hundreds — of soggy 5- and 10-dollar bills on Mrs. Gilmore's clothesline. Spread out on the ground beside them, several long rows of shoes were laid out in the afternoon sun to dry.

Just 24 hours ago, Bug couldn't wait to put this sleepy little village behind her. Now she found herself almost pleased by the prospect of resting here awhile.

Mrs. Gilmore joined her at the porch rail. "I told your father the two of you can stay with me for a few weeks while your collarbone heals. It'll probably take that long to get everything sorted out about the accident anyway."

Pointing to Frogger at the clothesline, she laughed warmly and said, "It also seems that my yard is going to be recovery central for a while. People just keep showing up with wet money and dripping shoes." She gave Bug's shoulder a gentle squeeze. "Will you stay?"

"Sure. I'll give it a try," said Bug. "For a while." And she had a small smile on her face as she stared off across the lawn full of her new neighbors.

The Author and the Illustrator

Frank B. Edwards spent 16 years living with his family in a small, friendly village that was very much like Tichburg. Their 150-year-old house overlooked a tumbledown dam that served as the village swimming hole, and they spent many summer nights on their front porch listening to the water rush over the falls. Each September, they attended the Centreville Fall Fair the weekend before school started.

A former magazine editor and feature writer with *Harrowsmith* magazine, Frank started writing children's books in 1990 and has more than 24 to his credit.

These days, he lives beside a small, quiet lake between Kingston and Ottawa.

Illustrator *John Bianchi* is also a children's author and has worked with Frank since their magazine careers crossed paths in 1980. Since 1986, they have created almost 40 children's books together, even though they now live 3,000 miles apart. One of John's best-known books is *Snowed in at Pokeweed Public School*.

You can contact John and Frank at: mail@Pokeweed.com

Frogger by Frank B. Edwards

Frogger is the first book in *The Adventures of Bug & Frogger* series. Nominated for the Ontario Library Association's Silver Birch Award when it was first published in 2000, *Frogger* explores the life of young Frogger Archibald, who lives in the sleepy little village of Tichburg — population 473.

Tichburg boasts 27 volunteer firefighters, 4 fire trucks, 3 small stores and a cast of offbeat residents who make life interesting for an energetic, curious 11-year-old boy who tries to help everyone he meets.

Frogger's neighbors include:

Cigar Davis, a crusty 85-year-old who returns to Tichburg and finds a lost childhood treasure.

Dolly Gilmore, the elderly fire chief who keeps an eye on the village from her big front porch.

The terrible Troth twins, Kenny and Kerry, who defy the efforts of Tichburg's best babysitters, including Frogger.

"There is good stuff in Frogger . . . This is the world of Henry Huggins, Robert McCloskey's Homer Price . . . a very comfortable place to be."

Sarah Ellis, Quill & Quire